ANISHA

ACCIDENTAL DETECTIVE

Name: Anisha Mistry (I do have a middle name but it's too embarrassing so I am **NOT** writing it here)

Age: 10 years, 3 months and 10 days (at time of writing this)

Lives with: Mum, Dad, and my mischievous Granny Jas

School: Birmingham South-West Aspire Junior Middle High Academy School (longest school name ever!)

Favourite Subject: Science

Best friend: Milo Moon

Ambitions: To meet a real life astronaut

To invent a cure for meanness

To be the first kid in space

For Rishen and Avni, who bring the sunshine even on the cloudy days xx
SERENA

For Davey G, as always
EMMA

First published in the UK in 2023 by Usborne Publishing Limited, Usborne House, 83-85 Saffron Hill, London EC1N 8RT, England, usborne.com

Usborne Verlag, Usborne Publishing Limited, Prüfeninger Str. 20, 93049 Regensburg, Deutschland VK Nr. 17560

Illustrations by Emma McCann.

A CIP catalogue record for this book is available from the British Library.

JFMAM JASOND/23 ISBN 9781805311935 9332/1

Printed and bound using 100% renewable electricity at CPI Group (UK) Ltd CR0 4YY.

CHAPTER ONE

FREEDOM!

It's the best day ever! Finally, freedom! Well, for the next few days anyway. We're going on our Year Six residential trip! For **THREE** whole days!

I was a bit nervous at first, just because I've never really been away from home without at least one of my parents or Granny Jas, but then Mindy, Manny and Milo got super excited about all the fun we could have, and that made me excited too. Plus, for the first time ever the residential is also doubling up as a science and geography field trip! Two subjects I really love!

Thirty of us are going to a place called Coral

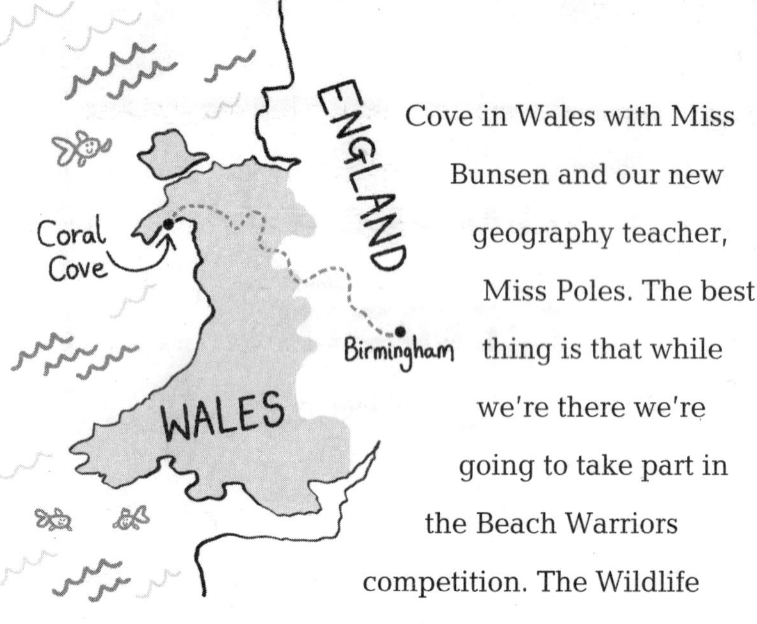

Cove in Wales with Miss Bunsen and our new geography teacher, Miss Poles. The best thing is that while we're there we're going to take part in the Beach Warriors competition. The Wildlife Protection Society is running a series of local competitions in certain parts of Wales to raise awareness of how we can all tackle beach pollution and look after our wildlife and nature. It's open to all the schools in those areas and Miss Poles thought we could do it as part of our trip! She had to check we'd be able to take part and The Wildlife Protection Society said we can!

To enter we have to come up with an idea for making a positive difference to or raising awareness about beach pollution. Miss Poles suggested cleaning up the beach and making our own wildlife habitats* there. We just have to take photos of our project and write some words about what we did and email it all in by four o'clock on Wednesday. There will be a winner for each town that is taking part and they get to name a section of beach where they do their project!

Anyway, it's exactly **7.32 a.m.** on Monday morning and we're standing outside school with our suitcases while Miss Bunsen checks everyone off on the register. I convinced Mum and Dad not to wait to wave off the coach. Even as we were saying goodbye at the car just now, Mum was lingering and being weird and looking at me with misty eyes.

"Ah, beta, I'll be right here when you come back, okay?" she said. "And don't worry if you need to come home early, Dad will hop in the car and come to get you."

"I'm not driving almost three hours to Wales!

*** A habitat is another word for the home or environment of an animal or plant.**

She'll be fine. You'll be fine, won't you, Anni?" Dad had ruffled my hair then.

My tummy had lurched. I was so excited, but Wales **IS** a long way from home. Mum must have seen that millisecond of doubt in my face, because then she offered the most horrific thing.

"I could come along with you! I'm sure the teachers wouldn't mind..."

"NO!" I shouted a little too loudly. "That's a lovely idea, Mum, but I think I'll be okay. It'll be good for me, you know! I need to be a bit more independent."

Mum hadn't looked that convinced, but thankfully Aunty Bindi had phoned her right at that moment, which distracted her. Every phone call from Aunty Bindi is exciting at the moment. The baby is due any day now. Aunty Bindi's tummy is so big, and sometimes we can see the baby jiggling about in there. The whole family is so hyped up about it, which is the other reason I'm sort of desperate to get away. That sounds horrible, but I don't mean get away from my family... Well, maybe a little bit.

I love my family, but it's a lot right now. Mindy and Manny are going to be a great big brother and sister. They've been helping Uncle Tony get the baby's room ready at their house. Granny Jas has

taken up knitting and is making all kinds of woollen things. Her first attempt was a bit wonky, so she made it into a big orange scarf and said it was for me! It was way too long, plus it's summer, but I didn't want to hurt her feelings so I wrapped it round myself three times and wore it to school. I thought everyone would laugh at me, but Beena decided it was cool and somehow I started a trend of wearing woolly scarves to school. It didn't last long once Beena realized it's far too hot and uncomfortable!

Granny also organized a special **pooja*** for the baby. A bit like a baby party, but weird because the

*** A pooja is a special blessing with prayers. Granny takes them very seriously. The main thing I know about poojas is that they involve a lot of sitting around with your legs crossed, which really hurts after a while!**

baby isn't here yet. Aunty Bindi and Uncle Tony had to sit on the floor with a priest who said lots of stuff I didn't really understand, but Aunty Bindi was really happy. Sometimes it feels like we have **poojas** for everything in our family! The only good part was that they had a massive chocolate cake afterwards!

Mum and Dad are super excited about the baby too. They've been cooing over tiny baby clothes, and Dad has been filming the family lots, so the baby can watch it when they're older.

I guess I've been feeling a bit...well, a bit like the spare tyre in the back of Dad's car. A bit not-needed. I don't really know what **I'M** supposed to be doing! That sounds really silly when I think it out loud, though, and I haven't told anyone that. It's supposed to be a happy time and it is. I think I'm just a bit overwhelmed and the beach trip will be a good break. **Won't it?**

Beena Bhatt's voice snaps me back to the current moment.

"Miss Bunsen, where shall I put my parasol and my deckchair?" she squeals.

I look over to see Beena wearing a full-on summer dress, sunhat and sandals. She's pulling a bright-pink suitcase behind her, and her mum is pulling along another two cases, with a deckchair and a parasol under her arm. Miss Bunsen looks worried.

"Er, Beena, we did say just one bag. And you won't need the deckchair or the parasol either. We won't really be sitting around on the beach."

Beena looks confused. "What do you mean? It's a beach trip, right? I packed my swimming costume, my best sunglasses, suncream…all the important stuff!"

Miss Bunsen sighs. "Did you read the letter, Beena? We have been talking about the trip in class. It's a research trip. There won't be any sunbathing, dear. We'll be building habitats, going for walks, climbing, and gathering samples of seawater and sand."

"URGH, YUK!" Beena shouts. "That

doesn't sound fun. Did you know about this?" she yells at her friends Layla and Amani, who also look confused.

Beena's mum sighs. "Oh, Beena. I did think it was a bit strange when you said the school was taking you on a seaside retreat. I wish you'd let me read the letters they send home!"

"It's **NOT MY FAULT!**" Beena screeches. "I don't want to go on this rubbish trip anyway now! It sounds **BORING!** Come on, Mother, let's go back to the car!" she orders.

Beena's mum laughs. "I don't think so, Missy. You've got clothes and your toothbrush; you'll be fine. It'll be an adventure! Off you go." And she nudges her towards Miss Bunsen. "I'll take the deckchair and parasol home with me."

Beena stands there in horrified silence as her mum marches away, and then Miss Bunsen herds her onto the coach. I stifle a giggle. Beena is much better than she used to be, but some things never change. I sit down near the big pile of bags waiting to go onto the coach and open my backpack to check I have everything. I've got three books, my notepad, pens and my favourite soft teddy that Aunty Bindi gave me when I was little. I rub its head and tuck it down in the small side pocket.

Just then Mindy and Manny arrive with Aunty Bindi. "Anisha!" Manny shouts out happily from under his huge backpack. It has all kinds of things hanging from it: a saucepan, binoculars, a torch, a bucket and a spade!

"Are you sure you have enough stuff with

you, Manny?" I chuckle. "You do know we're not camping outside; we will have beds to sleep in and meals cooked for us."

"I'm just being prepared!" he replies. "Besides, how many books have you got in that bag, Anisha?" he teases.

"Fair point!" I laugh.

"I did try to tell him," Mindy says. "You know how he loves all that survival stuff. Remember when we went on that forest holiday!" She rolls her eyes.

"Er, as I remember it, the walkie-talkies and secret signals worked very well!" Manny retorts. "And anyway, the bucket and spade are definitely necessary. I want to see if we can find the **secret sandcastles** on the beach we're going to. I saw a thing online and it's super cool! It went viral!"

Mindy sighs. "Is that the YouTube video you showed me?"

Manny grins. "Yeah! Anisha, wait till you see it. There's this person in Coral Cove – where we're going – and they leave these amazing sandcastles on the beach."

"Okaaaaay," I say, not sure what the big deal is.

"No, you have to see these sandcastles, Anisha!" Manny enthuses.

"They are pretty good, I suppose," Mindy admits.

"And," Manny continues, "**NO ONE** knows who is building them! How cool is that? I want to build a sandcastle next to one of the secret ones and take a picture!"

Aunty Bindi waddles up behind us. "Oh my darlings. Be safe, okay. I love you both **soooooooo** much!" She squeezes them. "And you too, Anisha, come here!" She yanks me into a big bear hug with Mindy and Manny and the baby bump.

"Now listen. Baby and I will be waiting here for you all, okay?"

"Don't come out yet, baby!" Manny instructs the bump.

"We'll call you!" Mindy says, waving her phone.

"I'm afraid not," Mr Graft, our head teacher, says as he walks past. "There's no phone signal where we're going. We'll post updates on the school website when we can, but no news is good news and you have the telephone number of the dorms we're staying at, in case of emergency."

He says the word **EMERGENCY** very meaningfully.

"What? But they'll be gone for three whole days!" Aunty Bindi shrieks.

"Don't worry. We'll find a way to keep in touch," Manny reassures her, and gives her a final hug.

Uncle Tony walks up with Mindy and Manny's cases. "Mindy, what is in this case!" he complains.

"Not much. Just a few clothes and all the snacks Bindi packed for us in case they don't feed us." Mindy smiles.

Uncle Tony chuckles. "She'd come with you if she could!" He turns to Aunty Bindi. "Right, shall we leave the children to get on their coach, sweetums? We have that medical appointment remember?"

"Oh I suppose so," she replies. "Be safe and stick together, okay?"

Aunty Bindi squeezes everyone one more time and then she and Uncle Tony leave. I can see Aunty Bindi looking back every few steps. We wave and smile till my face hurts.

"This is so awesome," Manny shouts once they're finally gone. "We haven't been to the beach in so long! I hope we get to swim in the sea. I brought my snorkel!"

"It's not the Bahamas. What do you think you're going to see in the sea, Manny, someone's old shoe? Anyway, where's Milo?" Mindy asks.

"I don't think he's here yet," I say, and then I see him. He's wearing his backpack, carrying a litter picker, a net and wearing a cap that says **TEAM GREEN**!

"What's all that for?" I ask.

"I'm doing my bit for the environment," Milo explains. "I watched this documentary about how

the wildlife on
our coasts is in
danger, because
of littering and
pollution. I want
to clean up the
beach!"

"Well, that's kind of why we're going there, Milo," Mindy points out.

"I know that," he answers seriously. "That's why I'm being prepared."

"That's exactly what I said!" Manny exclaims and they high-five each other.

Just then Miss Poles calls out, "Right, children, it's time to go. Shall we line up and get onto the coach in an orderly manner, please. No pushing. That means you, Oliver! Nice cap, Milo!"

Milo grins broadly. "Thanks, miss!"

We join the queue next to the coach, putting our

cases in the storage space under it. I notice a big brown suitcase with stickers on the front that say **India**, **USA** and **Kenya** on them. It looks really familiar.

"That's so funny. You know who has a bag just like that?" I say.

"Who?" Mindy asks.

"Granny Jas. It's like the one she took to India that time and came back with filled with mangoes and got into trouble at the airport."

"I'm surprised Granny didn't come to wave us all off actually," Manny comments.

"Yeah, me too. She was being a bit weird on the phone last night. Maybe she's sad we're going," Mindy says.

"I didn't even see her this morning," I say.

"She was probably too busy knitting for the baby." My voice sounds hard when I say that and Mindy looks at me inquisitively.

I change my tone. "You know, because it's not long till the baby comes now," I say brightly, wondering what that lurch was in my tummy. It's been happening a lot lately.

"SURPRISE!" a voice shouts out from the luggage compartment, and Granny Jas jumps out from behind the brown case!

"Granny!" I yelp as I fall backwards into Mindy.

"What? Were you really hiding in the luggage compartment? How on earth did you get in there?"

"Aw, you **DID** come to see us off!" Milo says happily.

"Nope." Granny grins as she reaches out for his hand, and he helps her out.

Something starts to dawn on me then, as I untangle myself from Mindy. That bag doesn't just look like Granny's bag; it **IS** Granny's bag! "Granny, why is your bag in the coach?" I ask.

"That's the surprise!" she laughs. "The school were asking for a volunteer to come and help chaperone you children, and I thought, what fun! I haven't been to the seaside in years. So, of course, I offered and they accepted...and now here I am!"

"OH, I,er... Wow," I say, suddenly losing all my words. I was not expecting this at all. I had gotten used to the idea that it was going to be a no-grown-ups week.

I look at my cousins. They don't seem bothered at all. "That's great, Granny," Mindy says, smiling. "Let me help you put your bag in here."

"Road trips with Granny are the best!" Manny beams.

"Do Mum and Dad know you're coming with us?" I ask.

"Ha, no! I left them a note and some paratha in the freezer. They would have tried to stop me. You know what they're like, **beta**. All that too-old nonsense they tell me. I'm looking forward to getting my feet in the sea, and won't it be nice for us to have some time away together!"

I force a smile. "Yeah, lovely, Granny." I don't know why, but I feel really irritated that Granny's here. Which is weird because Granny is one of my favourite people.

"You okay, Neesh? Your face looks strange," Milo says as we get onto the coach.

"I'm okay. I guess I was looking forward to it just being us," I whisper. "It'll be fine."

"Yeah, totally, and Granny **IS** a lot of fun," Milo reminds me.

As the coach pulls out of the school gates, starting the journey to Wales, I can hear Granny Jas behind me starting to hand out snacks. A few minutes later she's getting her knitting out and asking the other kids to help unwind her wool, while starting a singalong.

Everyone loves Granny. I love Granny. But right now, I feel really, really **ANNOYED**.

CHAPTER TWO

CORAL COVE

Three **LOOOOOONG** hours later, we arrive in Coral Cove, the place we're staying for the next two nights. As the coach turns a corner, we're suddenly faced with the sea. Everyone is **oohing** and **aaahing**. There's something about the sea that makes me feel calm and excited at the same time. I can feel myself relaxing: this trip is going to be just what I need right now.

After a few more turns, the coach pulls up in front of a dingy old building that has a big sign saying *Dankridge Dormitory* on it. Below that it says *B&B for schools and group bookings*.

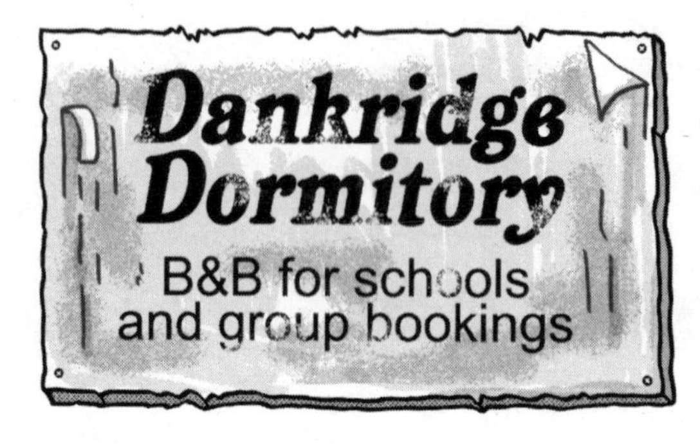

"Is anyone concerned that it's called **DANKRIDGE** Dormitory?" Beena shouts, standing up. "Hellooooo, 'dank' as in nasty!"

"Beena! Sometimes it IS okay to keep your thoughts to yourself," Miss Bunsen warns.

"Just saying!" Beena replies and sits back down. For once I kind of agree with her. This place does not look inviting!

We get off the coach and have to grab our bags and walk up to the shabby building, which Miss Poles calls the "Dorm". Apparently staying in a dorm means we have to share rooms with other people!

Mr Graft has already given us all a big lecture on the coach, about the kind of behaviour that is not acceptable while we stay in the Dorm.

The rules are:

- **NO** running
- **NO** shouting
- **NO** squealing
- **NO** pillow fights
- **NO** fighting of any kind
- **NO** staying up past 10 p.m.
- **NO** talking after lights out
- **NO** food in bed
- **NO** climbing of the bunk beds, unless you are sleeping in the top bunk. The bunks are **NOT** climbing frames.

The list goes on and on!

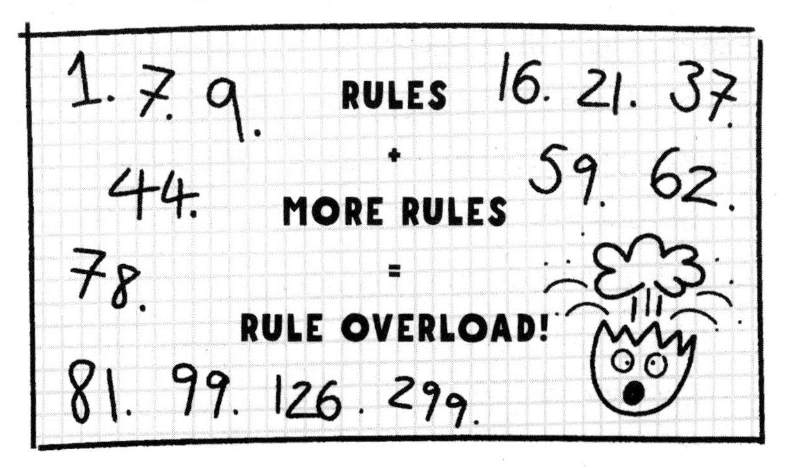

As we're walking up to the Dorm, Manny and Milo are chatting excitedly about their room and the people they're sharing with. They're already making plans for who gets top bunk and what scary stories they're going to tell.

A thought suddenly occurs to me. "Where is Granny going to sleep?"

"With you of course!" Granny grins, jumping up beside me.

"I, er, I don't know if that will be allowed, Granny. The grown-ups have their own rooms," I say, crossing my fingers. Sharing a room with my granny on this trip is **NOT** going to help my already non-existent level of cool.

Thankfully Miss Bunsen hears our conversation and confirms, "Yes, don't worry, Mrs Mistry. We've got a nice quiet room for you, away from the noise!"

"Oh, okay," Granny says, sounding **disappointed**.

I feel bad then. Granny really does want to spend

time with us and I'm being horrible. But I do just want some space. Is that bad?

I'm soon distracted as we enter the Dorm building. There's a slightly musty smell and our voices echo as we walk down a long hallway into the reception area. A man is standing behind the desk and although the sign in front of him says *WELCOME*, he doesn't look very welcoming or happy to see us at all. Mr Graft takes charge and explains who we are.

"We're the group from

Birmingham South-West Aspire Junior Middle High Academy School." He smiles broadly.

The man barely looks up. He types something into an old computer and hands a bunch of keys to Mr Graft.

"The rooms are upstairs. Breakfast is at seven o'clock and dinner is at six."

"Jolly good. We wondered if we might..." Mr Graft starts to say, but the man walks away without another word!

"Ah,er, he must be very busy. I'll catch him later," Mr Graft says. "Right, children, follow me!"

Milo nudges me. "That manager was rude. I wanted to ask what was for dinner today!"

"Maybe he was just busy," I say. "I'm sure we'll get a chance to chat to him later."

But as we go past the manager's office, I see the door is open just a crack. The man's face appears and then he slams the door properly shut.

We file up the stairs noisily. Everyone is chatting

and dragging cases behind them. As we get to the first floor, the teachers start sending groups into the different rooms. It's chaos and the hallway is packed full of kids, so Mindy and I stick together till we get to ours and then squeeze in through the doorway at the same time.

They've split the girls and boys into separate rooms. Mindy and I are in a room with six other girls. I like most of them, apart from Ella P – (there are three Ellas in our year!) – who used to be nice but then started hanging out with Izzie J and now I see them making fun of people in the playground, which I hate. Thankfully Izzie is not staying in our room. I know this because she's been complaining about it **LOUDLY** since we got the room allocations. We also don't have Beena in our room, which is a relief because I know she'd just take over all the space. There are six beds split into two bunks of three. I go on the bottom and Mindy bags the bed above me. Ananya, Roopi, Kimani and Ella P follow us in and pick a bunk each. I've never really hung out with any of them so it's nice to have a chance to chat. Turns out Ananya is really into science like me, and Kimani is into skateboarding, which Mindy has been wanting to learn. Even Ella seems much nicer when she's away from Izzie.

"I wonder who Beena is sharing with!" Roopi giggles.

"I feel bad for them, whoever it is!" Mindy replies.

We spend the next fifteen minutes figuring out what we need to take down to the beach with us. It's a warm sunny day, so we pack sun cream, hats and our water bottles. Manny pops his head round our door and offers to share his metal detector and a pocket-sized life raft. He assures us it will expand to proper size, but I'm not convinced it would work. Plus, I'm not sure we'll need a life raft. I hope not anyway!

Soon we hear Miss Bunsen and Miss Poles rounding everyone up to go out and explore for our first day. We only have till Wednesday and I'm quite excited to get started on our eco project. Granny Jas walks along with us and we talk about what we'd name the beach if we win the competition. Beena butts in and suggests "Beena's Beach" of course!

Manny comes up with "Survival Sands" and Mindy likes "Calm Cove".

We walk in pairs down into the town. Some of us pull along a trolley that has all the stuff we'll need for the project in it – buckets, spades and other tools. Beena tries to add some of her own beach stuff but Mr Graft glares at her and that stops that. It's only a

few minutes' walk till we reach the small promenade where there are a few shops: an ice-cream parlour, a souvenir shop and a chip shop. The smell of freshly fried fish and chips comes wafting out and makes my tummy rumble as we pass.

"Is it lunchtime yet?" Milo grumbles. "I'm hungry!"

"Not yet, Milo," Miss Poles says. "We'll have lunch on the beach, once we've made a start. Now, remember, we said there are four stages to our project. What was the first one?"

Milo looks confused.

"I remember," I say. "Are we tidying the beach first, so we have a clean space to work in?"

Miss Poles beams. "Yes, exactly right, Anisha!"

"And then we get to gather our building materials, right?" Mindy adds.

"Yes, and I have a list, a bit like a treasure hunt of things you might like to collect and use for your wildlife habitat," Miss Poles replies. "There will be a prize for anyone who manages to find everything on the list!"

"Ooh, I love treasure hunts!" Manny squeals.

"And then," Miss Poles continues, "once you have all your materials, you'll need to design your habitats. I know some of you have started this already in class and at home. Then, we can start building. You can work in teams or by yourself."

"Milo and I are going to make the most awesome habitat ever!" Manny brags.

"Really?" Mindy folds her arms. "And what type of animal is going to come and stay in it?"

"Any animal that wants to. All wildlife is welcome at mine!" Milo declares proudly. "We might put that on a sign on the front of it actually!"

"Umm, Milo, I don't think animals can read," Manny points out. Milo ignores him and carries on talking about the materials he might use.

"Will there be other schools doing their projects on the same beach as us?" I ask.

"Maybe, but I imagine as we're so close to the deadline a lot of people will have already done their projects," Miss Poles replies.

We walk a little further and we're soon at the beach! Miss Poles told us earlier that it's half-term here so it's quite busy already with families settled on blankets with picnic baskets and buckets and spades. Other people are walking their dogs. Children are chasing the tide as it goes out and running away as it comes back in. At first, I think how lovely it is that we're here, but I very quickly

notice the beach really is a bit of a mess! There are sweet wrappers and plastic bottles just thrown on the floor. An empty plastic bag rolls along across the sand in the breeze. The bin nearest to us is overflowing with rubbish, and then it looks like people have just chucked their rubbish near to it.

"I think we have our work cut out for us!" Miss Poles mutters.

CHAPTER THREE

THE BEACH

Everyone runs onto the sand eagerly.

Mr Graft shouts, "No running into the sea, please! Stay together. You boys! Are you listening to me?" and he marches off after the boys, who are most definitely not listening to him. A few parents sitting on the beach look our way disapprovingly.

Miss Bunsen plonks her bag on the sand in front of us. "Right, children, let's park the trolley and start tidying up. I have gloves and bin bags. Work in pairs or groups, please, and don't pick up anything sharp or alive!"

"Can we go for a swim later?" Manny asks.

"Er, I don't think so," Miss Bunsen answers.

"Aw, why not?" Manny moans. "I told Anil from the other class we could race each other. I know I'll be faster than him any day!"

Mindy nudges him. "The sea can be dangerous, Manny: currents, tides, big waves! You know, you can't just do what you want because Dad and Bindi aren't here. Good job I'm here, isn't it!"

Manny pulls a face at her and stalks off wearing big blue rubber gloves, with a bin bag flapping around in his hand.

"Do you like swimming, miss?" Milo asks Miss Bunsen.

"No, I er… Well, I never learned to swim, Milo. I'm not keen on the water, you see," Miss Bunsen answers sadly.

"Oh dear," Granny Jas says. "I could teach you if you like. It's so easy once you get the hang of it! I taught my son when he was little, and I taught Anisha too."

Miss Bunsen goes a little pink in the cheeks. "No, that's okay, Mrs Mistry. I wouldn't want to take up your time like that. Besides, the sea can be a little choppy and just as Mindy said, I'm not sure it's safe at all." Miss Bunsen's face looks a bit queasy and worried.

"Okay beta, don't worry. Listen, we can at least do something about this fear you have of the water. You know, just put your feet in and paddle about a bit!"

"Oh no, I couldn't, it'll be cold and...wet!" Miss Bunsen replies. "Anyway, we have to look after all the children."

Granny winks at me and whispers conspiratorially. "Just wait and see, I'll have her running about in the waves in no time!"

I look back at Miss Bunsen, who looks like she wants to run away as far as possible, and I think to myself: this might be Granny's biggest challenge yet. But I'm also secretly glad she's focusing on that and not me!

We spend the next hour collecting rubbish along the beach. We see some children building sandcastles and that sets Manny off looking for the **SECRET** sandcastles he's seen online. We don't find any but we do find bottle tops, plastic containers, scrunched up paper and sweet wrappers. We pick it all up and fill up two bags of rubbish. After an hour, the beach is looking much cleaner and we all decide to take a break and plonk ourselves down on the sand. Just then Beena, Layla and Amani walk past us towards the shoreline.

"Where are you going? Miss Bunsen said we need to stay this end!" I point out.

"You guys can do whatever. We're getting the best view of the sea and we can paddle our feet in the lovely warm water," Beena says, waving me away.

"Do you think she realizes we're in Wales and the water she wants to paddle in is the Irish Sea and probably freezing?" Mindy asks.

"Ha, no I don't think she does, but she's about to find out," I reply.

As we're sitting there in the sun, people-watching, Miss Poles drops her backpack down near us and starts taking out various bits of scientific equipment that look interesting.

"Are you making a habitat too, miss?" I ask.

"Sure, Anisha. I'm gathering samples of sand. Here, use this tool to scoop a small amount into each container. If there are bits of plastic or rubbish in the scoop, that's fine, put that in the container too."

"What's it for?" I ask.

"As well as teaching, I'm studying part time on a

special course in environmental science," Miss Poles explains. "These samples will form part of my project. I'm testing beach and sea pollution."

"That sounds like Anisha's dream course." Mindy smiles.

"She's right," I admit, "I want to be a scientist when I'm older."

"That's amazing, Anisha! Come and chat to me any time about science. I'm a geography teacher, but geography and some parts of science work really well together and can explain a lot of the world around us," Mis Poles replies.

"I'd love that!" I say. "I've never thought about how other subjects can team up with science!"

Just then we hear a squeal coming from the shore. It's Beena and her friends. They're hopping around barefoot in the shallows.

"**AAAAAARRRrrrghhhhhh!** It's freezing!" Beena screams. The water is only up to their ankles, but they are all flailing about and gulping air like fish, as if they are fully submerged.

"Help!" shouts Layla.

"Too **COLD**!" squeals Amani.

"Why don't they just get out?" Mindy asks. "They're saying it's too cold, but they're still jumping around in it!"

"Get out of the water!" Mr Graft shouts. "Get **OUT** of the water!"

"You'll have to go and help them, Miss Bunsen!" Miss Poles shouts. Miss Bunsen is nearer to the girls than we are, but she seems frozen with fear and is shaking her head.

"No. No! I can't do it. The water, the water!" she cries.

"I'll go," Mindy sighs, getting up.

But suddenly Granny Jas swoops over, runs across the sand like lightning and pulls all three girls by the hand, back onto dry sand.

Beena comes running over, shivering. "I need a towel. Someone give me a towel, I'm freezing!"

"You got your feet wet, Beena. The rest of you is dry, see, you'll be fine," Miss Poles tells her.

"Miss, I'm literally soaked, my hair is all wild from the wind and I just can't cope with these conditions!" Beena complains.

"Come here, beta, I'll get you sorted," Granny tells her as she pulls the girls along by the hands. "I have towels and my special home-made balm in my bag that will warm you all the way down to your toes!"

I try to signal to Beena not to do it but she doesn't see me. Granny means well, but all her home remedies taste **RANK!** I watch them walk over to where Granny has set up her things, pretty sure the girls will be running back this way again any minute soon!

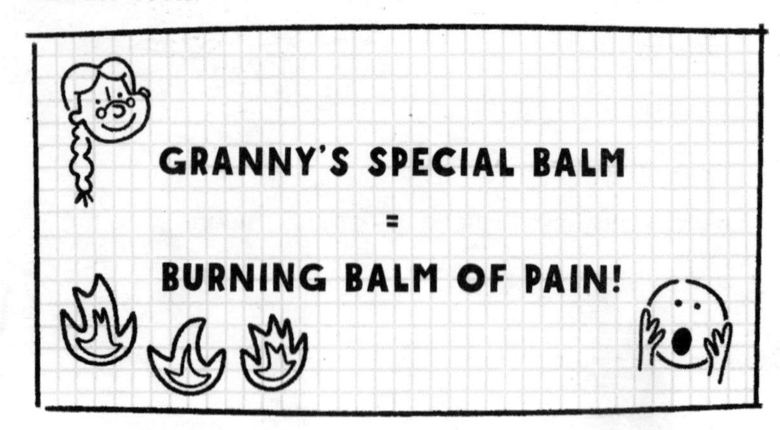

Miss Poles gets us to pile all our filled rubbish bags up and says we'll take them to the big bins across the road later. In the meantime, we eat our packed lunches. It's nice to sit in the sun and chat for a while. Mindy and I practise writing our names in the sand, and Milo tries to dig the biggest hole he can. Manny uses the pile of sand from the hole to make a hill and spends ages running up and over it until he trips and goes flying.

"Only you could hurt yourself on actual soft golden sand, Manny." Mindy sighs.

Manny pulls a face but then straightens up as Miss Bunsen walks past.

Mr Graft comes over then to see how we're doing.

"Aye aye, mateys!" he says, grinning. He's been talking like this for the last hour. I think he's trying to be a pirate."Did you know there are caves along this shoreline?" he asks us in a hushed voice, even though there's no one near enough to hear us.

"Caves? **Cool!**" Manny exclaims.

"Where? I want to see!" Milo joins in.

"I found a map online; we can go exploring!" Mr Graft says. "I loved exploring as a boy. I don't get to do it much nowadays. Plus, us Midlanders don't often get to be down by the sea, so I think it'll be a good educational experience."

"I don't like the sound of caves," Mindy declares. "They're dark, damp and sometimes there are **bears** in them!"

"There aren't any bears at the beach, silly!" Manny tells her.

"Don't call **ME** silly! I'm telling Dad!" Mindy shouts.

"Dad's not here!" Manny laughs.

"That's enough, children. Your parents aren't here but I am, so no bickering, okay?" Mr Graft interrupts. "Now, come on, me hearties!" he says saluting us.

Milo and Manny jump up straight away and salute him back. I look at Mindy. "It might be cool to explore a bit, and we can gather our bits from the habitat material treasure-hunt list along the way. I don't like dark places either, but we'd better keep an eye on those two. Who knows what trouble they'll get into!"

"I heard that!" Manny calls out from in front of us.

"You were meant to!" Mindy shouts back.

"What's going on with you two? You haven't stopped **bickering** all day," I say as we start walking.

"Oh, he's just getting on my nerves recently," Mindy moans.

"Really? I thought you lot were all happy families

right now, with the baby coming."

"Yeah, we are. I mean, we're excited but it's a lot, you know. I think we've all just had too much time together recently." Mindy sighs.

"Wow, I had no idea. I've been feeling a bit…" But I don't get to finish what I was going to say because Manny, Milo and Mr Graft have stopped dead in front of us.

"What is it?" I ask.

They move out of the way to reveal the biggest sandcastle I've ever seen. It has towers and turrets and a drawbridge and everything! It's so detailed!

"Wow!" I say as we watch people stop to take photos of it as they are walking past.

"Wow indeed!" Mr Graft whistles.

"Where did it come from?" Milo wonders.

A quiet voice answers from behind us: "It's the Secret Sand-Maker's work."

We turn to see who the voice came from. It's a kid around our age. He's on a bike and he's got a friend on another bike next to him.

"Who are you, and who is the Secret Sand-Maker?" Mr Graft asks them.

"I'm Danny and he's William. We live round here," the boy answers. "And the Secret Sand-Maker is, like, secret! That's the point, see – no one knows who they are!"

"And they just make sandcastles and leave them here," Manny adds. "I've seen them online. So cool!"

"Yeah, pretty much. Not just castles either. Further up the beach they made a sculpture of a ship like it was stranded! They're a local celebrity 'cept no one knows who they actually are!" The boy laughs.

"And, er, why aren't you boys in school?" Mr Graft asks sternly, looking them up and down.

"It's our half-term this week. Don't they have that where you're from?" the one called Danny smirks.

"Yeah, of course we do," Manny retorts. "Ours was last week actually!"

"And this week you thought you'd come and wreck our beach, did you?" the one called William asks roughly.

"What? No! We're here doing a project about the beach and how to keep it clean, and the environment and stuff!" Mindy answers quickly, looking very offended. "We've been collecting the rubbish off your precious beach actually!"

"Yeah, that's all we need, a bunch of outsiders poking their noses in," Danny answers. I get the feeling he doesn't like us very much.

I think Mr Graft does too, because he says, "Right, well, time to head back to our group, children. Nice to meet you, boys. Enjoy your half-term," and he marches us back to Miss Poles and Miss Bunsen and the others.

"Aren't we going to the caves?" I ask.

"No, we'll do it later," Mr Graft replies curtly.

"Isn't the beach for everyone?" Milo asks. "Why were they being like that?"

"Imagine if where we lived became a tourist attraction and it was just busy all the time with visitors," I say. "I guess it would get annoying after a while."

"I guess," Milo says.

"I'd love to know who the Secret Sand-Maker is," Mindy says.

"Me too!" agrees Manny.

I look over my shoulder at the secret sandcastle and I wonder why someone would do that, just leave random but amazing sand sculptures all over the beach and not want anyone to know they did it. Weird.

We reach the rest of our group just in time to see Granny trying to show Beena and her friends how to do cartwheels in the sand. As her sari flaps around in the wind, I'm very grateful I convinced her to wear leggings underneath it!

Just then something whips past me in the wind and hits my head. **Ouch!**

"What was that?" I shout. Then something else flies past me, and I realize it's a bit of rubbish, an empty crisp packet. Oh, there's a plastic bottle. And a can. Wait, what? Then I spot a black bin bag, just like the ones we just used to gather up all the rubbish. It's empty and it's rolling along the beach in the wind. All the rubbish that was in it is everywhere! How did this happen?

"Miss Poles!" I shout out.

Miss Poles is looking at some papers and fiddling with her hearing aid, like she does when she's concentrating. She hasn't noticed what's going on. She looks up and her face is suddenly panicked. We all chase around grabbing the rubbish. At least two bags have emptied out onto the sand, so it's not easy to collect it all up and get it bagged up again with the wind whipping the bits of paper and plastic up and around.

Eventually we stop, out of breath, and collapse on the sand.

"How did that happen?" Mindy gasps.

"I don't know, I don't get it. We tied the top of the bags, right? Look, most of them are still there, piled up," I reply.

"Maybe we missed those two and the wind knocked them over," Miss Poles suggests, sweeping her hair out of her face. "Or perhaps one of us kicked it over by accident?"

It doesn't seem right to me though.

Mr Graft runs up to us. "What a day it's turning out to be!" he huffs. "Can we carry on as planned, Miss Poles?"

Miss Poles frowns. "Yes, I guess the children could get on with their scavenger hunt."

"Good, let's get on then, shall we? A bit of wind won't stop us!" he replies cheerily.

"I, er, I'm not sure it was the wind," I say.

Mr Graft laughs. "Always looking for a mystery to solve, Anisha."

Just then a gust of wind whips Milo's cap away and he has to chase it down the beach.

"See, just the wind." Mr Graft nods. "Let's get to work, Anisha. Lots to do!"

I do as he says, but something niggles at my brain. I'm not quite as convinced as everyone else seems to be.

CHAPTER FOUR

MEETING MR WRIGGLES!

With most of the rubbish gathered up, we finally set about searching for the things that are on our scavenger list for habitat materials. Miss Poles gives us clipboards with the lists on and pencils to tick things off as we find them.

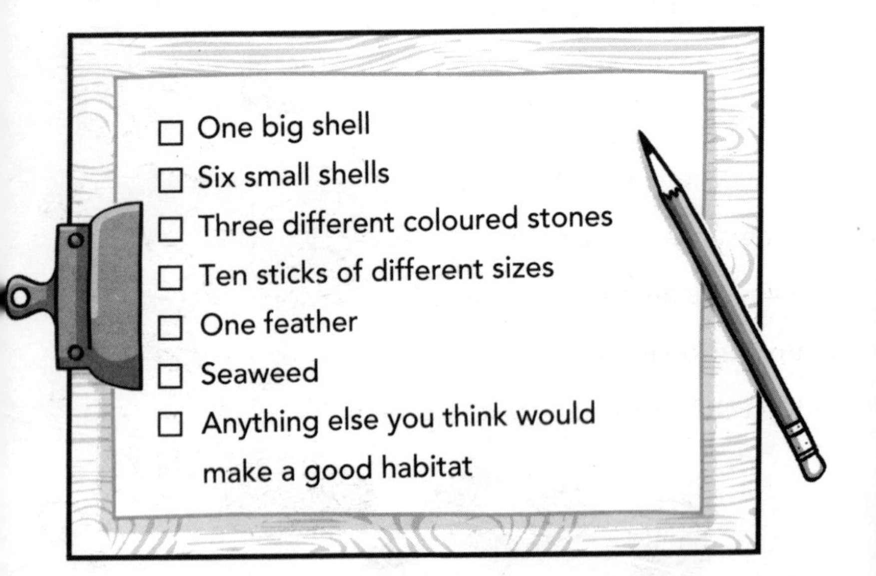

Things get really competitive from the start. Max Jones, Dean Mahmood and Imtiaz Khan start chasing each other with big sticks. Beena Bhatt marches around pointing at shells on the ground and shouting at Layla and Amani to pick them up. Miss Bunsen tries to call out positive encouragement, but she gets drowned out by all the shouting!

"Over here!"

"Hey, that's my shell, I saw it first!"

"My rock is bigger than yours!"

"Ew, get that seaweed away from me!"

It's chaos. Mindy and I break away from the group and find a quieter space to forage in. I look for the perfect shells and pebbles to decorate my habitat with. I'm going to line them up outside to make a path, so the wildlife know they're welcome.

Milo wins the scavenger hunt of course. Mindy and I make a pile of our collected things, and then Manny and Milo join in too. Miss Poles sees our pile and says what a good idea it is to keep everything together. When we've finished, she gets everyone else to put their stuff with ours.

"I don't think we'll fit all that in our trolley, and it doesn't make much sense to lug it all up the hill to bring it back tomorrow," she says, "so we'll leave it here tonight. It's far enough away from the shoreline so the tide won't be a problem. We could do with covering it over till we start building tomorrow."

"You can use my red blanket to cover everything!" Milo offers. "I was going to use it to sit on the sand, but it will cover the wood and twigs really well. Look, it has loops on the corners so it's perfect for putting tent pegs through."

"If you're sure, Milo," Miss Pole says.

"Yeah, I don't mind." Milo smiles. "It's a really good one, my mum got it for me."

So we use the blanket to cover the building materials and fix pegs through the loops at the corners to secure it into the sand.

We even scribble *Please do not move* on a piece of wood, as a sign, so anyone coming across it knows not to disturb it.

"That should be nice and secure overnight," Miss Poles says.

We head back to the Dorm, and the grumpy manager we met this morning is there. I notice now that he has a name badge which says Mr Coast.

"Afternoon!" Mr Graft offers cheerfully.

"Afternoon," Mr Coast replies. He's not smiling, but at least he responded this time.

"We've just been down to the beach, it's awesome!" Milo says happily. "You must just love living here. Do you go to the beach every day? I would if I lived here!"

Mr Coast stares at Milo. "I **NEVER** go to the beach. **EVER**," he replies, and he walks away towards the kitchen.

He was strange and rude, I think to myself.

"Oh, er, I didn't mean to upset him," Milo says.

"It wasn't your fault; you were just being friendly," Mindy says.

"Yeah, don't worry about it," I say.

"Maybe he's scared of the beach, like Miss Bunsen," Manny offers.

"I'm not afraid of the beach, just the sea," Miss Bunsen calls out from behind us.

"What are we doing now?" Beena whines. "My legs hurt, I need a hot bath!"

"There are no baths here, Beena," Miss Poles informs her.

"**WHAT!** How are we supposed to wash? I can't be smelly. That is **NOT** going to happen," Beena shouts. Here she goes again!

"Calm down, **beta**, there are showers," Granny

Jas tells her. "You know, in India when I was a girl—" but Beena cuts her off.

"Showers! Well, I hope they're the powerful ones like we have at home. Ours is like a rainstorm!"

"More of a rain trickle," someone says. I look and it's a girl I don't recognize.

"Er, you're not from our school," Beena says rudely, before she marches off up the stairs.

"Sorry about her," I say to the girl, who just looks amused.

"Ha. Well she wasn't wrong, I guess. I live here. My dad's the manager," the girl holds out her hand. "My name's Livvy Coast."

"Is your dad always that grumpy?" Mindy asks. I nudge her in the side. "Ow, Anisha!" She glares at me. "But he is!"

Livvy laughs. "Yeah, I guess he is kind of grumpy. I'm just used to him, I suppose. He wasn't always like that."

"Why doesn't he like the beach?" I ask.

Livvy's face changes then. "Oh. Because he used to go there a lot with my mum, but that was a long time ago."

"Oh," I say, not wanting to ask any more, because I can tell there's something sad behind what Livvy is telling us.

"Anyway, how are you guys enjoying Coral Cove?" she asks us.

Livvy tells us about the Dorm and the local area. She promises to show us the ice-cream parlour tomorrow. We tell her about our project and what we did today.

"Oh yeah, our school was supposed to be taking part in the Beach Warriors competition but then half-term came and we hadn't done anything for it. I think some of the local kids were trying to get something together, but I haven't heard much," Livvy says, looking sad for a second, then she smiles again. "Beach clean sounds fun."

"Yeah, we met some of the local kids. William and Danny," I say. "I don't think they liked us being on your beach."

"Ah, don't worry too much about them. They mostly just skulk about and ride up and down the beach on their bikes. They just like looking moody and annoyed." Livvy laughs. "They're basically harmless."

After chatting for a while and then going up to change and wash our hands, it's time to go for dinner. Livvy comes with us and shows us the way. As we enter the dining room, Mr Coast is there. He frowns at first but when he sees Livvy he breaks into a smile! They hug and Livvy introduces us to him.

"Dad, these are my new friends, Anisha, Milo, Mindy and Manny."

"Ah, er, yes…I think we met earlier. Sorry for being rude," Mr Coast apologizes. "I'm sure Livvy has told you I can be a bit grumpy when things are busy here. Can we start again?"

"That's okay. It's nice to meet you properly," I say.

"Please, take a seat and enjoy dinner. We've got pasta bake and garlic bread today!"

"Ooh yum, garlic bread!" Milo grins and rubs his tummy.

Just then a little ginger cat saunters into the room and rubs itself against Livvy's leg.

"Oh wow, you have a cat?" Milo asks.

"Yeah. Well he's the only ginger cat in our little town, which makes him kind of special, so he gets fed by everyone!" Mr Coast explains. "His name is Mr Wriggles because he never sits still and if you try to cuddle him, he wriggles away. He wanders off all the time. I hardly ever know where he is or what he gets up to. We usually have to just follow the trail of ginger furballs and shedded cat hair to find him!" He gives Mr Wriggles an affectionate pat.

"I like him," Milo says, kneeling down to stroke Mr Wriggles. The cat looks up at Milo, yawns and then strolls away.

"We'll catch up later! I'll be just over here!" Milo calls out to him, but the cat ignores him.

"Don't take it personally, he's like that with everyone," Livvy tells us. "He'll come back when he's hungry!"

We line up to get some food and then find a table to sit down. Mr Coast joins us.

"So, how are you finding Coral Cove?" he asks.

"It's so cool," Milo says.

"We really like it. We went to the beach and saw the secret sandcastles!" Manny adds.

"I don't get all the fuss about the sandcastles," Livvy says quickly, looking at her dad.

Mr Coast looks all serious then. "Well, you know,

each to their own. If you'll excuse me, children, I feel a headache coming on."

"Is he okay?" I ask Livvy, once her dad has gone.

"He doesn't like to talk about the beach or sandcastles, ever since my mum left," Livvy replies. "It's just a thing with him."

"Our mum left too," Manny says, "but our dad met Anisha's aunty and now they're married."

"Yeah. I don't think my dad would ever get married again," Livvy says, staring down at her food.

"So what else is there to do around here?" I ask brightly, trying to change the subject. I can tell she doesn't want to talk about her dad any more.

"There's the roller rink," Livvy says.

"As in, roller skating?" I ask. "Oh no, I'm not doing that. Mindy and I had a bad experience on roller skates!"

Miss Poles comes over to our table then. "This seems like a lively table. Mind if I join you?" she asks.

"We're just talking about other stuff to do in

Coral Cove," Mindy explains.

"It is very pretty here..." Miss Poles nods. "I bet there are some great walks."

Manny laughs. "We were thinking more along the lines of arcades, miss!"

"Are there any wildlife sanctuaries here?" Milo asks.

"Not really, unless you count the woman who keeps seagulls in her garden," Livvy jokes.

"Seagulls are very misunderstood you know!" Milo says wisely. "I read that they're actually very

clever creatures. They can learn and even teach other behaviours! And they have excellent vision."

"Yeah, but they're also quite scary," Mindy says. "Remember that time when there were some in town and that big one was trying to get your chips?"

"He was just very hungry and we had a bit of a misunderstanding," Milo replies.

"Ha, he almost landed on your head!" Mindy laughs.

"Well, anyway, I think it's nice what that woman is doing for the seagulls. We could all do a bit more for our local wildlife. Right, Miss Poles?" Milo asks.

"You're so right, Milo," Miss Poles agrees. "That's why I'm trying to do my research while we're here. I'm fascinated by the effects of tourism and pollution on our beaches. Tourism is obviously good for business in towns like this, but sometimes it has a negative effect on the local wildlife and nature."

"That's really interesting. I'd love to know more about your research, miss. I read a book last month about the effects of pollution on our climate and the environment."

"Ooh, you'll have to show me it when we're back at school, Anisha. Well, I want to look at how dire the situation is, so we can get some funding to raise awareness. Competitions like the one you're taking part in are great for that, but to really get businesses and councils to take notice we need some hard evidence!"

"Like what, miss?" I ask.

"Well, I'm collecting samples of seawater so that we can test for chemicals and other residue. And we can take photos of rubbish on the beach and how it impacts the wildlife. I'd really like to conduct a full survey, but it takes time and I need funding to come back and do it properly. The people who have the money need convincing that this is an urgent priority!" She shrugs.

"What could be more urgent than this?" I ask, thinking about all the rubbish we collected earlier.

"I'll help you gather evidence," Milo offers. "I've always wanted to be an eco-warrior, working to save the world!" He stretches his arm out like Superman.

"I'll help too!" Manny offers.

"We all will," I say.

"I might go down to the beach for a walk later," Miss Poles says. "I'll see if I can find a good spot for us to set up the samples."

Livvy frowns. "Oh, no one goes down to the beach at night-time, Miss Poles. There isn't much lighting down there, so it's hard to see the shoreline. Best not to wander around in the dark."

"I hadn't thought of that. You're right, it can wait

till morning," Miss Poles replies.

Just then Mr Wriggles the cat jumps onto our table and sits on Milo's plate.

"I guess he does like you after all!" Livvy laughs.

"Er...I know I said I wanted to be friends, but could you get off my pasta bake?" Milo asks.

Mr Wriggles just meows and turns away.

After dinner, someone suggests we go to the lounge and play some board games. It's a bit difficult to play a game with so many of us, so we break off into groups. Some play cards, some play chess and someone tries to start a game of Monopoly, but since everyone in their group wants to be banker, they spend the whole time arguing about that!

Granny Jas starts a game of charades with her group. It's weird seeing my granny playing with other kids. I don't know why, but it makes me feel funny. Lately nothing feels like mine any more. I know I didn't want Granny to come on the trip, but now she's here it's weird having to share her. I rub the thought out of my mind.

Stop being overdramatic like Beena, I tell myself. Then Granny starts telling stories of when I was little, and gets out her mini photo album, which is super embarrassing! **WHY** would she bring that with her? Everyone is shrieking with laughter at the photo of me walking around in my nappy, and I just want to shrink myself till I'm invisible.

This trip is slowly turning out to be a nightmare!

I opt out of the games and ask if I can go to another room and read instead. It's getting so noisy in here now. I grab my book and go back to the now-empty dining room, which overlooks the beach.

I sit by the window and look out. It's pretty much pitch black outside now, with only the odd street lamp lighting up the road. It seems like here the town gets super quiet in the evenings. There aren't even any people walking past outside.

Then I notice a light, down where the beach is. It's small – like a torch maybe – and it's moving across the sand. Who would be down there in the dark? How strange!

Just then Mindy and Livvy come to find me.

"Why are you in here all alone?" Mindy asks. "Come and play Battleships with us!"

"Oh, no thanks, Mindy. I'm going to sit with my book for a bit. It's been a hectic day; I just need some quiet time," I explain.

"Yeah, of course. Just come find us if you change your mind, okay?" Livvy smiles.

"I will," I promise.

As soon as they leave the room, I go back to looking out of the window, but the moving light has gone. Maybe I imagined it!

An hour later and it's bedtime. Which is of course chaos. I'm glad I had some quiet time with my book, because there's no chance of it now!

Everyone is charging in and out of each other's rooms. I can hear Beena making demands for a softer pillow and asking why there isn't a lamp by her bed. Miss Bunsen rushes from room to room telling everyone to calm down, but no one really listens. Mr Graft has his stopwatch outside the bathrooms and tells us we each have three minutes precisely to go to the toilet and brush our teeth.

Even with the timer, the queues for the two bathrooms are painfully slow, and by the time I get to brush my teeth the sink is full of toothpaste and the toilet roll has all finished. I guess this is what it would be like if I had lots of brothers and sisters.

I drag myself back to our room and I can hear Granny Jas saying goodnight to literally everyone as they get into bed. I crawl into my bunk, exhausted and annoyed. Eventually, Granny Jas pops her head in through our door. "I just came to say goodnight, **beta**."

"Night, Granny," I say, not turning round to face her.

"Everything okay, **beta**?" she asks.

"Yep," I say.

"Sure?"

"Yes, sure."

I feel Granny hug me from behind, but I don't hug her back. At home I would definitely, but here it feels odd and I'm really aware of my friends in the room. I pat her hand and huddle under my duvet more. She says goodnight to my friends and pads silently out of the room.

"You sure you're okay, Anisha? You don't seem yourself," Mindy whispers in the dark.

"I'm fine. I wish everyone would stop asking me," I snap, swallowing hard.

What **IS** going on with me? I feel like there's a big knot inside me, all twisted up and I can't untangle it.

I close my eyes tight and hope the knot will have gone by the morning.

CHAPTER FIVE

DISASTER STRIKES!

The next morning, we all sleep in till half past eight. I'm so tired. Last night I barely slept from all the noise of the others shuffling around in their beds. I'm not sure who it was but someone was singing in their sleep in the room next to us and it kept me up for ages! Now, as I drag myself up, my eyes are droopy and feel like they need propping open with sticks. Although that would hurt quite a bit, I imagine!

Miss Bunsen walks in and calls out, "Morning, sleepyheads, rise and shine! We have a lot of work to do today!"

We have our breakfast down in the dining room. Everyone is here except Miss Poles. Maybe she overslept. But then after a few minutes, she comes in from outside. Her hair is all windswept and her cheeks are very red. She rubs her hands together and blows on them like you do when it's very cold.

"Are you okay?" Mr Graft asks in a concerned voice.

"Oh, I'm fine! I went for a jog!" Miss Poles beams. "Sea air is good for the lungs!" she puffs, as she leans against the wall for support. "It's just a smidgen windier than I expected, that's all!"

After breakfast, we grab our coats because it looks a bit overcast and head out. Mr Graft says he'll catch up with us, as he wants to go for a jog now too. What is it with all the grown-ups wanting to run? They never seem in this much of a hurry back at home!

I notice it's not that windy now as we leave the Dorm – maybe it's calmed down since Miss Poles went for her jog. Everyone is excited to start building our habitats. As we start walking down to the beach, Milo tells us he found a piece of wood that he's planning to paint his sign on. He's even looked up the word **WELCOME** in Welsh* – which is **CROESO** – and he's going to write it in both languages! Mindy has gathered some bits of material to make a soft bedding area for hers. Manny is planning to build the tallest habitat possible, with several floors.

"Birds can fly in at the top floor and land animals like crabs and lizards can go in at the ground levels

***Welsh is one of the oldest languages in Europe! We tried to learn some in school. Did you know that beach in Welsh is "traeth"?**

and the first floor!" he tells me happily. "What's your habitat going to be like, Anisha?"

I shrug. "I'm not sure. I was thinking of maybe an underground habitat, but I don't know if it will work. I have an image in my head but I feel like it's going to be hard to make it real, you know?"

"Underground sounds awesome, Anisha, and so thoughtful! There are creatures like crabs that like to stay under the sand, so it would be perfect for them," Manny replies. "I get what you mean about vision versus reality, but I bet it'll be amazing."

"Thanks," I say. "I'm excited to get started. I can't wait to see them when we've all finished; it's going to look so awesome!" We're all super excited, chattering and laughing all the way down. Until we get there.

Miss Bunsen seems to have stopped up ahead, and someone cries out. "It's **GONE!**"

I move to the front to see what's happened.

It's a **DISASTER!**

The pile of materials we left under Milo's blanket has gone! The wood, sticks and bushy branches we'd worked so hard to find – even my pebbles and shells – they've all disappeared! The blanket too. All that remains is a shred of fabric caught in one of the tent pegs we used to secure it.

Beena yells, as she marches her way to the front too. "What is going on?"

As she's barging through I think for a split second I see some words scrawled in the sand. Does that say **GO AWAY!**?

I try to look closer but Beena stomps right through it and it's gone.

"Did you see that?" I ask Mindy but she says, "What, Beena? Yeah, drama as always!"

Miss Bunsen scratches her head. "Are we sure we left everything here?"

"Yes, it was definitely here. Look, you can see where we poked the pegs into the sand to secure Milo's blanket over them," Mindy says.

"How can this be?" Miss Poles asks, as she takes it all in too.

"Maybe the wind swept it all away, like it did with the rubbish?" Miss Bunsen replies. "You did say it was windy earlier, when you came out for your jog. Did you go past here at all?"

Miss Poles frowns. "No, I ran in the other direction. I should have come and checked everything was okay." She wanders off, distracted.

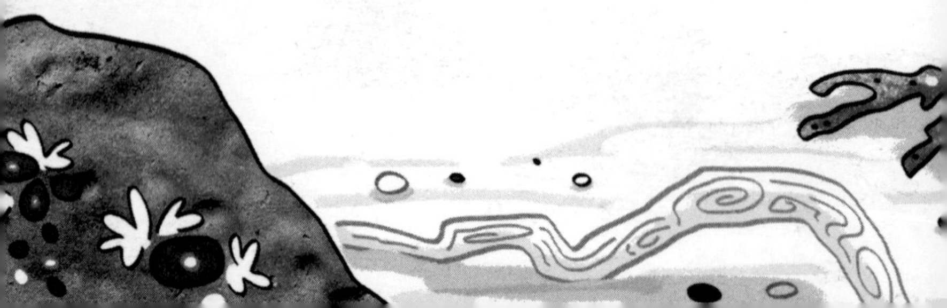

"No, it's not your fault. It's no one's fault. Just an accident, I'm sure," Miss Bunsen calls out after her in a reassuring voice.

"But, miss," I say, "I'm sure I just saw someone had written in the sand '**GO AWAY!**'"

Miss Bunsen peers over her glasses. "I can't see anything, Anisha. The beach is full of people," she says, gesturing around us, but the beach is actually much quieter this morning. "They would have seen if someone did this deliberately. Come on now, children, chin up. It's never as bad as it seems," she continues.

I shake my head. "I can't believe this. My pebbles and shells... I found the perfect ones to make a path leading up to the habitat," I whisper sadly. "I bet I won't find any nearly as nice as those now."

"We worked so hard!" Milo says. "I had the perfect sticks! I'll have to explain to my mum about my blanket as well. Does this mean we have to start all over again?"

"I'm afraid so," Miss Bunsen tells us. "It won't take us long, if we all pull together. Come on, the quicker we start, the quicker you can all begin building your wonderful habitats."

We split off and start gathering bits of wood and rocks again. No one is excited this time, just fed up and disheartened. Milo and Manny head in one direction while Mindy and I stay this end.

"This is annoying," Mindy says. "I was looking forward to getting started on the building bit!"

"I know," I agree. "Me too. It **IS** strange that we seem to keep having problems though, isn't it? First all the rubbish we collected supposedly blows away in the wind, even though we were pretty careful about tying the tops and putting the bags neatly in a pile. Then we get over that and start collecting our building materials, but as soon as we turn our backs they disappear! We made sure we secured them with the blanket and those pegs stuck right down in the sand. How did the wind move them?!" I wave my hands about. "A bit suspicious, don't you think?"

"What are you saying, Anisha?" Mindy asks. "You think we're being sabotaged?"

I shrug. "I don't know for sure, but something's going on. I can feel it."

"Okay, well you usually have good instincts so I'm with you. But what can we do about it?" Mindy asks.

"Let's have a look at the site of the missing materials. There might be a clue!" I say.

We creep around on the sand on tiptoes and try to look for any evidence. It's a bit pointless though, as everyone has already trodden through there. But then, just as I'm about to give up, I see something. It's so small I almost miss it.

"There, look. Is that…a paw print?" I say.

"Where?" Mindy squints and kneels to look.

"There, see it?

"Are you sure it's a paw print? It just looks like a round dent in the sand." Mindy shrugs.

"No, there's more, look closer… See there, the hair – is that a ginger furball?"

"Ew, gross!" Mindy shouts, jumping back.

"Remember what Mr Coast said about the Dorm cat, Mr Wriggles? He has to follow the trail of furballs and ginger cat hair to find him!"

"You think Mr Wriggles did this? I guess cats can drag stuff with their mouths, but…"

"I know it sounds a bit far-fetched." I nod. "But it's a lead, and we have to follow it up. Let's keep looking. If this was the work of Mr Wriggles, then he couldn't have gone far with all our stuff. He's not a superhero cat!"

"Okay, well let's see if we can spot any more gross cat hair or furballs, I suppose!" Mindy cringes. "This is the most disgusting clue we've ever had to follow!"

"Look, there's one," I say, "and more paw prints!"

We follow the trail across the beach, but it soon stops. "Now what?" Mindy asks, looking around.

I'm about to say I don't actually know, but then I spot something.

Just a little way away from us there's a bush sticking up between two rocks. I can see a flash of red.

"Mindy, look," I say. "The blanket of Milo's that we used was red, wasn't it?"

"Yeah, I think so. Why?"

"Because look at that bush – look at what's caught on it." I point.

We run over and kneel down to see properly. It's a scrap of material that looks really familiar. It's from Milo's blanket!

"How did this get here? Could someone have been dragging the stuff and got the blanket caught on the bush?" Mindy asks.

"Maybe they did have to drag it. It was quite a lot of materials, it would have been heavy. What if the materials are still here somewhere, nearby?" I say.

"Let's look around. Manny, Milo, come here and help us!" Mindy calls.

Manny and Milo come running over and we show them what we've found. We all set to looking for the missing materials.

"There's a few bushes and big rocks over there. Let's try there first," I say, pointing to an area just a few metres away.

We pass Granny Jas and Miss Bunsen. Granny is talking about imagining yourself as the waves and swaying back and forth. Miss Bunsen looks like she might throw up.

We keep going, a few more metres down the beach. I just know our building materials – including my pebbles – are here somewhere. That huge pile can't just have disappeared.

And then I see another flash of red, this time poking out from behind a large boulder. I look around to see if anyone is watching us. There's no one about apart from our group. I run over to the boulder.

There's a big bush behind it but a gap to the side that's large enough for me to crawl round. I get on my hands and knees and shuffle forward enough to get my head into the space. I can't believe I'm doing this, but I need to get to it.

More red blanket! I pull on the end of the fabric and out it comes, dragging with it bits of wood and feathers and beach plants – everything that we gathered yesterday…and my pebbles!

"It's all here!" I shout out. "Miss, look what I found!"

Miss Poles comes running over. "What is it, Anisha?"

"Our missing materials. They didn't get swept away in the wind!"

Miss Poles frowns. "How? I mean, wow, that's brilliant!"

Mindy, Manny and Milo come over too. "Neesh, you found them!" Milo shouts. "You were right and you saved us all a load of time collecting new stuff for the habitats!"

Beena comes wandering over. "Urgh, Anisha. Do you have TWIGS in your hair? We don't all have to crawl through that hole, do we, miss? I'm NOT doing THAT!" she cries and runs away.

Mr Graft arrives, looking very refreshed and happy.

"What did I miss?" he asks brightly.

A short while later we've distributed all the materials again and **FINALLY** we're starting to build our habitats.

I need to start digging a hole to base the habitat for crabs in, but my mind keeps wandering. I can't stop thinking about how we found our stuff hidden away in that bush behind the boulder. They definitely didn't get there by accident; someone didn't want us to find them. The paw prints and the ginger furballs led us part of the way. Could a cat really have done all that, though? My mind goes back to Mr Wriggles and how Mr Coast said he never knows what the cat gets up to. He's the only ginger cat in town. Could it be him? But cats can't write the words "Go Away" can they?

One thing's for sure, someone or something doesn't want us to build these habitats. And I will find out **WHO** or **WHAT** took our stuff.

CHAPTER SIX

AN EVEN WORSE DISASTER!

We make good progress with our projects in the morning. All over our little section of the beach, habitats are coming together. It's like a little wildlife sanctuary, a village for our animal friends. Milo gets excited when a small beetle comes scurrying up to his animal hotel. The beetle has a look around and then hurries away.

"I bet he's gone to tell all his beetle friends about the hotel and they'll be back later!" Milo grins, and pulls something out of his bag. "Look, I have the perfect thing for when the birds come to visit. My Nan gave it me from her garden."

"What is it?" I ask.

"A birdbath!" Milo places it carefully near his habitat. "The birds can come and cool off here on a hot day! And look, it has a little bell that rings when they fly in."

"That's pretty cool." I smile. "Your nan always gives you the nicest things."

Meanwhile, Beena is still refusing to do any sort of work. She's lying on a blanket, while Layla fans her. Amani is standing in front of her positioned in a star shape, providing shade.

"Left a bit!" Beena orders. "No, right a bit. Stick your arm out more!"

"Why do they listen to her?" Mindy asks me.

"I have no idea," I admit. "I thought she was trying to be a bit nicer recently, but this trip seems to have brought the worst out in her again!"

Just then Livvy comes running down the beach.

"Hi, everyone! Dad sent me down to say lunch is ready, if you guys want to take a break."

"Ooh, I'm so hungry!" Milo says.

"Me too actually!" Mindy agrees.

"I'll join you back up there. I have to run a couple of errands for my dad," Livvy says and she runs off in the direction of the shops.

I realize I'm hungry too. All this thinking and digging is hard work! I'm a bit worried about leaving our habitats, but Granny Jas and Miss Bunsen say they'll stay back to keep an eye on everything and they can come up for lunch when some of us are done. That makes me feel better about going, so we put down our tools and leave everything as neat as we can. Milo has painted his wooden sign for his hotel. He props it up next to a nearby rock. It looks so good!

"I'm so excited to come back and finish this off!" he shouts. "This is the best project we've ever done!"

We head in for lunch and I eat, like, five sandwiches, before I start to feel a bit ill.

"I overdid it," I groan.

"Really?" Milo says. "I had six sandwiches and I'm fine. I might get another, actually..."

Manny beckons Mindy. "Shall we do it now, sis?" he whispers.

"Do what? I ask.

"We're going to try and call home," Manny explains.

"How? You heard Mr Graft – no phone signal, no contact with home," I say.

"Yeah, but there's a computer in the manager's office. We can do a video call from there," Mindy says. "Dad showed us how. He has this account he uses for work sometimes. Manny has the login.

I really want to check in on the baby."

"Okay, but we can't just wander into Mr Coast's office and use his computer!" I say.

"We can if he's distracted!" Manny grins.

"I can help!" Milo offers. "I'm good at being distracting."

We finish our food and check Miss Poles is busy. She's leaving the dining room and waves, saying she's got some work to do in her room and she'll meet us back down here in thirty minutes to go back to the beach.

It'll be nice to see Aunty Bindi and Uncle Tony, but I realize part of me doesn't want to call home. I'm not sure why. I shake it off though.

We leave the dining room and head towards the manager's office. As we go round the corner, we almost walk straight into Mr Coast!

Milo takes his opportunity. "Oh, er, Mr Coast, I had a question about the history of this building! Can you help me?"

Mr Coast looks like he'd really rather not stop and talk to anyone right now, but with a sigh he says, "Okay, what did you want to know?"

Milo grins. "Well, I noticed…" and he gestures behind his back for us to leave.

"We'll catch you later, Milo. We're going to head back to the beach now," I say, crossing my fingers behind my back. I don't like lying but I know how

much this call home means to Mindy and Manny.

Once Mr Coast and Milo are out of sight, we run the last bit to the office. The door is unlocked, thankfully, and we quickly step inside and shut it behind us.

Manny goes behind the desk and starts tapping away at the computer.

"Do we need a password?" Mindy asks.

"No, I was worried about that but it's already logged in," Manny says. "I just need to get into my account and we can call home. Hopefully Dad answers!"

"He's always on his laptop or phone. I'm sure he will," Mindy replies.

It seems like it's taking for ever, and I'm worrying the whole time that Milo will have run out of things to ask Mr Coast and then we'll get caught in his office!

"Hurry up, Manny!" I whisper.

"Going as fast as I can," Manny answers. "Here. Look, I'm in. Calling Dad now."

The computer makes a ringing sound and after about five seconds Uncle Tony answers.

"Manny, Mindy, Anisha, it's you! I'm so glad you called. We're missing you. Wait, exactly **HOW** are you calling me?"

"Don't worry about that, Dad, you knew we'd find a way!" Manny laughs.

"Well just don't get in trouble while you're there, please. But it is so good to see your faces. Are you okay?"

"Yes, Dad, we're fine. How's Bindi?" Mindy asks.

"I'm here!" squeals a voice next to Uncle Tony, as Aunty Bindi's beaming face pops into view.

"Mindykins! Mannykins! Anni! Oh, look at you all. Did you grow since I last saw you?"

"We're sitting down, how can you tell?" I say.

"Oh, my Anni, so clever. It feels like it's been weeks since you were all at home. How long left now?"

"We've only been gone one night!" I laugh.

"How's the baby?" Mindy asks.

"Oh, the baby is doing just fine, although I wish they would stay still for just a minute at least!" Aunty Bindi laughs, rubbing the bump.

Just then Mum and Dad come on screen. "Anni!" they shout a bit too loudly. What are they doing there? I turn the volume down on the computer. Someone is sure to hear them from outside the office!

I wave awkwardly. I don't like talking through a screen, it feels weird. No one else in my

family thinks so, but I just can't get used to it.

"Is Granny there?" Dad asks. "We got her note about secretly chaperoning. I'm not happy – tell her I'm not happy!"

"She's not here, Uncle," Manny says. "She's down at the beach. I'll tell her, but you should know she's having a great time. Everyone loves her!"

Dad huffs. "Well, that's great, but she didn't need to sneak off like that."

"I think she left you some paratha in the freezer," I say.

Dad's face lights up. "Oh really? I'll have some for my lunch!"

"So what have you all been up to?" Uncle Tony asks, as he gets nudged to the side by Aunty Bindi.

"Oh, well we've been down to the beach. We saw some boats, I wish we could go on one! Anyway, then we tried to build some habitats, but someone sabo—"

I nudge Manny before he can finish. They don't need to know about all that! Aunty Bindi will drive down here if she thinks there's any sign of trouble. She gets very protective of us. A bit too protective sometimes!

But it's too late, because Aunty Bindi has already latched onto something else Manny said.

"Did you say **BOATS**?" she asks in a high-pitched voice. "What kind of boats? A rowing boat? **NOT** a speedboat?!"

"They're quite big boats – I mean, there are small ones too – but we haven't been on any boats, so there's no problem. Don't worry," Mindy assures her.

"Yeah, they look **SO** cool, and I saw on one boat it had life jackets for emergencies and everything." Manny interrupts.

"WHAT! EMERGENCIES!" Bindi shrieks. "My babies... Tony, you need to drive me there now. They're going in the open water, there could be sharks or – what was that movie we watched? – The **MEGALODON!** What if that's in the water?"

Uncle Tony looks alarmed. "No, sweetums,

calm down. It's no good for you to get this upset."

Mum takes over then. "Bindi, get a hold of yourself. There are no Mega-Londons in Wales. London is miles from Wales, for a start! Plus, you heard Mindy, they haven't actually been on a boat yet."

"YET!" Bindi screeches. "Tony, get the car!"

Manny snorts. Mindy rolls her eyes. I cover one ear and mute the call with the other hand while Bindi shrieks. I can see Dad standing up, trying to calm everyone down. Mum's waving her arms about like a bird and Uncle Tony is holding his head in his hands. It's sort of funny to see them like this on mute, but also any chance of a normal conversation

But Mr Wriggles ignores me completely. Actually, he's crouching low to the ground, his ears are pulled back and he's hissing. I remember Milo telling me this is what cats do when they're scared. What is he so afraid of? I look around and then I realize. Mr Wriggles is afraid of the pile of sand!

But…if Mr Wriggles is afraid of sand, then he couldn't have been on the beach, dragging away our bits of wood and pebbles and leaving paw prints and ginger furballs behind. But he **IS** the only ginger cat around here, so that must mean...he was **FRAMED!**

The call draws to an end and we say goodbye to everyone. Mindy and Manny are so happy they got to see the baby moving around in Aunty Bindi's tummy.

As soon as the grown-ups have ended the call, I tell Mindy and Manny what I've found.

"I knew it couldn't be Mr Wriggles!" Mindy says, sounding relieved.

We sweep away the sand and give Mr Wriggles a reassuring pat. He meows, and scarpers out of the room.

We rejoin Milo outside. Thankfully Mr Coast has gone.

"How was your call?" Milo asks, as we head back out to the beach with Miss Poles and everyone.

"Dramatic!" I say.

"Loud," Mindy adds.

"Funny," Manny laughs.

"Aw, sounds great and very **Mistry-ous!**" Milo grins.

"Good one!" Manny snorts. "Although we're not Mistrys, technically."

"Oh yeah!" Milo smiles. "I always forget. Does that mean the baby won't be a Mistry?"

"Yeah, the baby will have our last name – Singh – of course!"

That makes me feel a bit funny again, so I change the subject.

"I can't wait to get back to our habitats. Hopefully things will go right for a change," I say brightly. "Oh and Mr Wriggles is in the clear, Milo. He didn't take our stuff."

Milo punches the air. "**YES!** I knew it!"

"We still don't know who did though, so we have to stay vigilant," I say. "I have a feeling this isn't over yet."

My fears are confirmed as we're walking onto the beach and we hear a scream coming from the direction of our base. It's Miss Bunsen! Granny is hopping up and down and pointing.

"What happened?" I shout as we run over.

But then I see it. My heart sinks and my tummy lurches.

Milo cries out, **"NOOOOOO!"**

Our habitats are **DESTROYED**. Milo's lovely sign is broken in half, his structure all trampled over and in pieces. My hole is all filled in with bits of rubbish, and the wood I was starting to use as the walls of my habitat has all been snapped. All the other habitats have been pulled apart and scattered across the beach. There's rubbish **EVERYWHERE!**

All that work. **GONE**.

The lovely clean beach, **TRASHED!**

Then Milo whispers sadly, "Where is my nan's birdbath?"

DESTROYED PROJECT

+

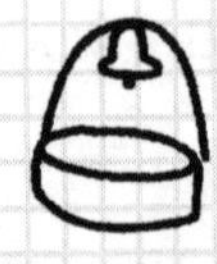

STOLEN BIRDBATH

=

MAJOR DISASTER!

CHAPTER SEVEN

BEENA SEES SOMETHING!

It's mayhem. All the kids are running around all over the place, shouting, crying and yelling at each other. Most of the tourists who were here earlier seem to have gone and the ones who are here didn't see anything. How could someone just come along and trash our project like that?

Milo just kind of sits there looking upset. Anything his nan gives him is really precious, and I know the birdbath was special.

"We'll find it, Milo," I say, patting him on the shoulder, but it doesn't feel like it's enough.

Miss Bunsen and Miss Poles try to gain control

but fail. Then Mr Graft comes along and booms his loudest head-teacher voice at everyone.

"**STOP** what you're doing, right now!"

We all freeze.

"How did this happen? Miss Bunsen, you and Mrs Mistry were meant to be keeping an eye out," he asks sternly.

Granny Jas wrings her hands. "It was my fault. I wanted to encourage Miss Bunsen, with her fear of the water...and she's been doing so well. We thought we'd go and stand by the water's edge; we only turned our backs for a few minutes. I just don't know why anyone would destroy all our hard work like this!"

I can see how upset Granny is so I go and put my arm round her.

"It's okay, Granny, we know you didn't mean for this to happen. We'll figure it out," I say, even though I have no idea how.

Mr Graft tells us to work in groups and try and see what we can salvage from the broken habitats – and make yet another pile of stuff that we can still try to use. He goes up the beach talking to the few people who are around. I can see them shaking their heads. No one saw anything and everything we had achieved so far is in ruins.

We start digging around in the mess to try and find Milo's birdbath, and I notice those local kids from before. They're lurking by the wall next to the beach. They glare at us and I glare back.

Then a grown-up with a clipboard comes over to them with some other kids, and seems to shuffle them all along. Looks like they're on some sort of half-term activity.

The grown-up points to the beach and he seems to be giving them a talk. The kids all look bored. If they hadn't been so rude to us, I might have invited them to help with our project!

Just then, Beena comes past complaining loudly.

"This trip is **sooo** boring! I suppose you lot think it's all mysterious and exciting, though."

"Not really 'exciting', Beena," I say. "Milo's really upset!"

Beena stops. "Oh, well yeah, obvs. But, like, you'll figure it out, won't you? You always do."

"We have no clues," I say. "Nobody saw anything, and there's no real evidence of who might have ruined our habitats."

Beena thinks for a moment and then starts jumping up and down. "I did, I saw something!"

"You did?" Mindy asks disbelievingly.

My ears prick up. "What did you see, Beena?"

Beena grins like a Cheshire cat. "Isn't this something. I've got information you want!"

"Beena, just tell us what you saw, or else," Mindy warns.

Beena huffs. "Oh, Mindy, chill! I'm only messing. So serious!" She flicks her hair, then leans in. "So,

I was trying to find a good sunbathing spot earlier. It's really difficult, you know! Anyway, I had just found a lovely sunny place and I was just laying out my blanket, the pink stripy one… anyway, as I was doing that someone barged past me. Practically knocked me over actually!"

"Who?" I ask.

"Well I don't know who they were!" Beena shrugs.

"Great!" Mindy rolls her eyes. "How is that helpful, Beena? That could have literally been anyone. It could have been me for all you know! It's not like you're that good at noticing other people, is it?"

"Hang on," Milo says. "Beena, was there anything about them that made you think it might be important to tell us?"

Beena grins again. "Yes! And actually, Mindy, for your information, I am very observant. For example, I notice you are quite rude! **ANYWAY!** The reason I know that the person who almost knocked me over was not from our group and was definitely suspicious is because of what they were wearing and carrying..."

Mindy looks at me. I look at Milo and Manny. Could Beena actually have a proper clue for us?

We all lean in. Beena whispers, "They were wearing joggers."

I frown. "Huh? Joggers. That's what made them seem suspicious?"

Mindy sighs loudly. "Beena!"

"Hang on, I'm not done!" Beena says, with a glint in her eye.

"Okay, why was the fact that they were wearing joggers suspicious?" I ask.

"Joggers by themselves aren't suspicious as such," Beena says, with an air of fashion wisdom. "I mean, I wouldn't be seen wearing joggers outside of my house, but, you know, it's a choice. However, who would wear joggers and then be carrying a very formal blazer to wear on top?" she shouts triumphantly.

We all look at Beena in silence, trying to make sense of what she's told us.

"It's a bit weird, right, Neesh?" Milo asks.

"I'm not sure," I say. "Beena, where did the person go after they almost knocked into you? Did you see if it was an adult or a child, a male or female? Anything else you noticed?"

"**SO** many questions! So just to be clear, they knocked me over. You said knocked into me, that's not right." Beena corrects me. "And no, I didn't see much, it all happened so quickly. I really only saw the back of them. I tried to talk to them, but they ran away and disappeared!"

"Disappeared?" Mindy scoffs. "How?"

"Well, if I knew that then I would have found them and told them off for knocking me over and not apologizing, wouldn't I!" Beena shouts.

I step in between them. "Okay, let's think this

through. Beena, when exactly was this?"

"Right after we came back from lunch, when everyone was yelling about the habitats being broken or whatever." Beena shrugs. "Oh, and weirdly as they ran past me I heard a jingling noise! Like a bell or something."

Milo and I look at each other. "The bell from my nan's birdbath!" Milo exclaims. "They were running away because they were the one who destroyed our habitats!"

"Beena, think carefully – where was the last place you saw them?" I ask her.

Beena points behind us. "Over there."

I look at the others and we all start to run in that direction. "Thanks, Beena!" I shout behind me.

"Whatever!" she yells back.

We run a short way, till we reach some rocks. I look around. Where could the mysterious person in the joggers and blazer have gone to from here? It looks like a dead end.

"Could they have climbed over?" Manny asks.

"No, it's too rocky and dangerous," Mindy points out.

"What's behind there?" I ask, pointing to some big shrubbery. Mindy goes to look.

"Come and see!" she shouts. "There's a path!"

We push our way past the shrubs, which are not as spiky as they look! There's a path under our feet!

We keep going. On the other side of the shrubs there's an opening and more path!

"Where does it lead to?" Milo asks.

"Let's find out!" I say.

We run up the path as fast as we can. It's steep and we're all out of breath when we get to the top.

"Oh, it's the Dorm!" I realize, looking up at the big building in front of us.

"So, whoever knocked Beena over ran up here?" Milo asks.

"Maybe," I say.

"This mystery is too confusing!" Mindy says, scratching her head.

We walk back down the path to the beach and sit on a big rock. I pull my notepad out of my bag. "I need to organize my thoughts," I say. Then I see the map that Miss Poles gave us yesterday with our scavenger list. I take that out instead.

I mark up the map. "Here's where we collected all the rubbish and it got emptied out and I'm sure someone had written 'Go Away'. Here's where we started building our habitats. Then the path is over here, and the Dorm is way up here,"

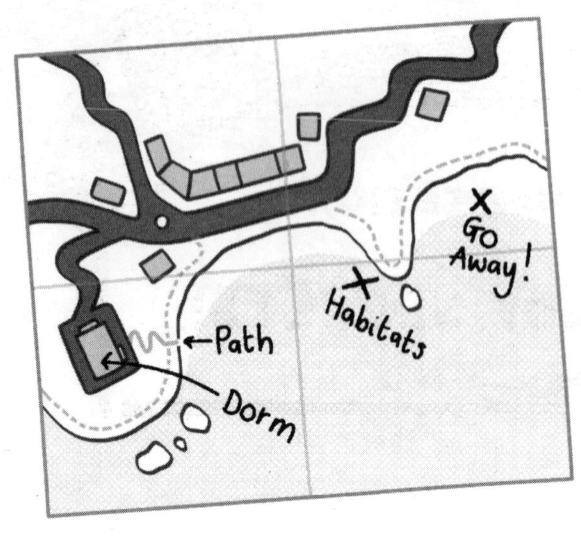

I say. "We know Mr Wriggles didn't do it. So we need to be on the lookout for other suspects now, and we need to be super vigilant around our habitats."

"Why would they take my nan's birdbath?" Milo asks.

"I'm not sure," I say. "But, Milo, I promise we'll make this right. Whoever did this is not going to get away with it." I hold Milo's hand tight. "We haven't found the right clue yet, but we will."

CHAPTER EIGHT

SANDY SECRETS!

We go back to the beach and search for Milo's birdbath, even though we know it's probably not here, since Beena heard the bell near the hidden path. With every section of the beach that we cover, Milo looks more and more defeated.

"I hate this," I say to Mindy. "Poor Milo, he's gutted."

"I know," Mindy agrees. "We'll get it back for him, though, won't we?"

"I hope so. I've promised now and I don't break promises," I say, looking suspiciously round at the beach and everyone on it. Someone here knows something. I just need to figure out who.

We clean up as much of the broken habitats as we can and start to rebuild. I begin looking for some new shells and for a moment, I think I've found a big pink one like the one I had before, but when I lift it out of the sand it's broken. If only we knew who was behind all this! I try to push the investigation out of my mind: we have to make some progress on this project. It's only when I hear Granny talking to Miss Bunsen about being excited to have another grandchild that I realize I haven't thought about all that baby stuff all day! This trip has been a distraction but maybe not in the way I thought it would be.

I notice Miss Poles hasn't moved yet and is staring at the sand and muttering to herself while she fiddles with her hearing aid. She looks… annoyed.

"Miss Poles, are you okay?" I ask.

Miss Poles looks up and stares at me. "Oh, er, sorry, what?"

"Are you okay?" I repeat.

"Oh no, that's fine, I just,er...I have to go and make a call, I've just remembered," Miss Poles explains, and she hurries off in the direction of the Dorm.

Teachers are so weird sometimes.

The time goes by really quickly and by teatime I am ready for a rest. It feels like today has been a lot! I think we're all feeling tired, because our whole group is quiet on the walk back to the Dorm.

We don't know who is sabotaging our habitats but I'm sure that they're close by, so we have to be vigilant! We cover over the parts of the habitats we rebuilt with a big plastic sheet that Mr Graft bought from the local hardware shop. This time we make sure to weigh it down at the edges with the heaviest rocks we can find. I'm still not sure it's safe but it's the best we can do.

We're taking our remaining materials with us, so nothing can happen to them. Mr Graft said he's asked Mr Coast if we can keep it in the hallway at the Dorm. Our trolley is piled high with sticks, stones and dry wood.

Tomorrow we'll spend the whole day finishing

our build. Miss Poles said the deadline for the competition is four o'clock. I just hope we can finish without anything else going wrong!

Dinner at the Dorm today is waffles and fish fingers and beans. I hate beans! The other choice is peas and I don't like those much either. Pudding is jam roly-poly, though, and that's one of my favourites. Livvy comes to sit with us and I tell her all about our afternoon: how everything got ruined, the path we found and the person in the joggers who almost knocked Beena over.

"That's so strange!" Livvy says. "Might just be a coincidence though."

"Maybe. Just from what Beena said, I feel like it's more than that," I reply.

"Yeah, but you said yourself Beena can be dramatic." Livvy smiles.

"That is true." Mindy nods.

"Who's dramatic?" Milo asks, with a mouthful of waffle, just as Beena walks past us.

"No one!" I say, smiling sweetly at Beena, who basically ignores us.

"So, what's the plan for tomorrow?" Livvy asks. "I guess there's no point in carrying on if there's someone out to ruin it, right?"

"No way, we're not giving up," Milo says firmly. "We promised the animals we'd build them a nice habitat, and that's what we're doing. This person, whoever they are, isn't going to stop us."

Livvy smiles broadly at Milo. "Then I'd love to come and help, if that's okay with you?"

"That would be great!" I say. "We'd really appreciate it."

Just then Mr Coast is passing our table. "I'll need you here tomorrow, Livvy," he says. "We have to do some homework."

"It's the holidays, Dad!" Livvy moans.

"Yes, but we need to keep your brain active. You want to go off and be something great in the world, don't you! Maths is important for that," Mr Coast tells her. "Besides, you know how I feel about the beach. No arguments. Tomorrow we're looking at fractions!"

Manny and Milo pull a face at each other – they hate fractions!

As Mr Coast strides away, I notice his boots leaving a trail of sand. How strange. I mean, we all have sand on our shoes, but that's because we've been on the beach. Mr Coast said he never goes down there.

I remember how I saw the small pile of sand in his office earlier too.

My detective brain kicks in, and I realize I need to get a closer look, but I can't say anything in front of Livvy.

Once he's gone, Livvy groans and puts her head on the table. "So annoying!"

"Why is your dad so set on homework?" Manny asks her. "Our dad's a bit like that, but even he wouldn't make us do fractions in the holidays!"

"Oh, he just doesn't want me to end up staying here in Coral Cove for ever. The town is so small and he says I could travel or live anywhere in the world other than here," Livvy replies. "He has this saying, 'Education is your passport out of here, Livvy!' I know he means well, but I kind of like it here. I don't know why he would want me to go somewhere else!"

"Maybe he just wants to see you do well," I offer. "Grown-ups have a funny way of saying things too. You should hear some of my dad's sayings!" I grin.

Livvy laughs. "Parents, right!"

"Grown-ups are weird," Mindy agrees. "Our dad has loads of sayings too. He thinks he's so wise, but then he'll do something silly like brush his teeth with some of Bindi's face cream by accident, because the tubes look similar. Remember when he thought mango and passionfruit was a new toothpaste flavour, Manny?"

Manny laughs. "He's started quoting from that baby book he's been reading now too. Something about babies are like angels or flowers or something!"

"Aw, that's cute!" Livvy smiles. "Are you excited to have another cousin, Anisha?"

I just nod and change the subject.

We finish tea and Livvy goes off to her room to get a head start on the homework, so she can try to convince her dad to let her come out with us even for a little while tomorrow. Manny and Milo start playing cards with some other kids. I grab Mindy and we go to the lounge.

"I think I might have a new suspect," I whisper.

"Who?" Mindy asks.

"Mr Coast. I don't know for sure, but something is definitely off. Earlier I saw sand in his office and again just now on his boots. He said he never goes down to the beach, so what's that about?"

"Ooh, that **IS** interesting!" Mindy agrees. "Oh...but that's Livvy's dad, and we like her."

"I know," I say. "But if he is the one destroying our project over and over, then we need to know. To prove it either way, I need to get back into his office. I feel like I've missed something in there that might be a clue."

"But he's in there right now, working. I heard him say to Miss Bunsen that's what he was off to do."

"You could distract him!" I say. "Tell him you need some help with fractions."

Mindy pulls a face. "Really? That's the best you can come up with? Fractions! Shouldn't we grab Milo and Manny to help?"

"No, it'll draw too much attention. And it might be nothing. I don't want to get Milo's hopes up that his birdbath is in there. I only need a few minutes. Please?" I plead.

"Oh, alright. Come on then!" Mindy groans. "I can do fractions myself, you know! I hate having to pretend to not know what something is."

"I know. You're super smart, which is why you can pull this off," I say. "And if we solve this mystery, then the rest of the trip will be so much better!"

Mindy grins. "Yeah yeah, okay, you've convinced me."

We sneak away to the corridor just outside Mr Coast's office. I can see light from under the door but it's awfully quiet.

"Do you think he's fallen asleep?" I wonder.

"No, it's only six thirty!" Mindy says.

Mindy knocks on the door lightly. No answer. She knocks again, harder this time. No answer.

I give the door a gentle push, and it swings open. The room is empty!

"Oh, he's not here!" Mindy exclaims. "Does that mean I don't have to do the whole fractions fake-out?"

"He might come back any second," I say. "Keep a lookout and I'll go inside to see what I can find. If he comes you'll have to ask him about fractions, but don't let him come inside this room, okay?"

Mindy nods. "Understood, captain!" She laughs and salutes me like Mr Graft's been doing to us all morning. I can't help but smile. Right, on to serious detecting business.

I go inside Mr Coast's office. Even though we were in here earlier, I make sure to look at everything carefully this time. I don't want to miss a vital clue.

I walk over to the desk. There's not much on it, just the computer, a notepad with some scribbles on and a photo frame. The photo is of a young man and a young woman. I recognize the man, it's Mr Coast but a long time ago. They're sitting on the beach and they're smiling; they look so happy. They're digging a hole in the sand with a bucket and spade. So Mr Coast did used to love the beach! I wonder what changed. I remember how sad Livvy looked when she said her dad didn't used to be so grumpy about it. Poor Livvy.

I look around the office once more and see another trail of sand leading to a big cupboard in the corner of the room. Maybe Milo's birdbath is in there!

I slowly turn the handle on the cupboard door

and reveal… Nothing, it's empty. But there is a sandy shape in the bottom corner of the cupboard – two shapes actually. They look like footprints. Like it's where a pair of boots are kept. And next to it there's a space with sand marking out a round shape like a bucket. But if those things are not here, does that mean Mr Coast is wearing them? Maybe he's gone back to the beach?

I have to get down there and see what he's doing.

I run out of the office and grab Mindy.

"What's going on, did you find anything?"

"We need Granny," I gasp.

"Why?"

"I'll explain on the way; we need to get there and we need to get there now!"

"Get where?" Mindy asks as we run down the hallway.

CHAPTER NINE

M.O.P.

A few minutes later Granny Jas, Mindy and I are running towards the beach.

Granny has come out with her quilted jacket on, carrying a torch and a tote bag.

"What's in the bag?" I whisper as we run.

"A rope, an emergency flare and some plasters," Granny says, sounding very matter-of-fact.

"What? Where did you get a flare, and why do we need it? What exactly do you think is going to happen to us?" I ask worriedly.

"Just a precaution. Best to be prepared!" Granny says seriously.

"It's only down this way. I don't think we're going to get lost," I say. I do pull my jacket round me a bit tighter though.

"Feel like explaining why I'm running in my sari towards who knows what?" Granny huffs.

So I explain to Mindy and Granny about the photo and the sandy boot prints. "He's clearly lying about never going to the beach. Maybe it's so we don't suspect him of sabotaging our habitats!"

"I knew there was something about him," Mindy says.

"Did you really?" I ask.

"Well, no, but that's not the point. The point is we have to protect our project, we're not going to let him go down there and ruin the bit we've rebuilt! If he is the one, we're going to catch him in the act!" Mindy says, punching the air.

"Well, we don't know anything for sure, so we need to follow and observe **FROM A DISTANCE!**" I say carefully.

"I've always wanted to make a citizen's arrest!" Granny yells, jumping up as she runs.

"Granny, what did I just say?" I whisper-shout after her.

We approach the edge of the beach carefully. There is a light moving around on the sand, just like the other night when I was looking out of the window! Someone is there. What are they doing? It's hard to tell who it is, but suddenly the face turns and...it's Mr Coast!

"Come on," I say. "He might be messing with our habitats. We have to stop him!"

We run over and pounce.

"Stop what you're doing! We know exactly what you've been up to!" I shout.

Mindy jumps in front of me in a karate pose. "We're serious – we know basic self-defence and we're not afraid to use it!"

"I don't know basic self-defence and neither do you," I whisper.

"He doesn't know that," Mindy mutters under her breath. "Fake it. Plus we have Granny, that's better than any training!"

Granny lifts her tiny fists and says, "Don't move a muscle, mister!"

Mr Coast lifts his hands in the air. "I give up! You've caught me."

He turns slowly to face us fully and moves to the side. My heart is pounding. Then I see what he is standing in front of. It's not our habitats at all. It's the beginnings of a...**SANDCASTLE!**

"Wait, what?" Mindy starts.

"It's a sandcastle," I say, stating the obvious.

Mr Coast smiles. "Yes, it's a sandcastle. You've caught me. I'm the Secret Sand-Maker."

I try to take it all in. Then I burst out laughing. "You are? Of course you are! It makes sense now!"

"It does?" Mindy asks, confused.

"Yes, the photo on the desk – when you were younger. You've always loved making sandcastles!" I say.

"You're very talented!" Granny Jas comments, as she examines the sandcastle. It's not finished but already the detail is amazing. I can see where he's started to carve out a bridge and the edges of the brick walls.

Mr Coast looks sad. "Thank you, that's very kind. Yes, I, well, we – my wife and I – we used to make sandcastles together. But then she left and now it's just me and Livvy, and I didn't want to make them for a long while. Then one day, I came down here when it was quiet, and I finally wanted to make one again. I left it, and suddenly everyone was making such a fuss about how good it was. It brought so much joy, but I couldn't face the attention, so I guess that's how I became the Banksy of the beach!"

He chuckles.

"It really wasn't meant to be this much of a thing! But wait, what did you think I was doing down here?"

My face goes hot as I realize I had it all wrong. "Well, someone has been messing with our project and destroying the habitats we've been trying to build," I say.

"And you thought it was me?" Mr Coast asks. "I feel like I should be offended!"

"Sorry," Mindy and I mumble.

"Well, maybe I can help you figure it out," Mr Coast offers kindly. "I love this beach and I don't like to think of anyone destroying any part of it."

We sit down on the sand and I explain the clues we have so far: the message in the sand, the person who knocked into Beena, the path to the Dorm.

"I thought I saw someone down here last night with a torch, but I guess that was you," I say with a sigh.

Mr Coast frowns. "Last night? No, that wasn't me. I really did go to bed with a headache."

"Wait...if it wasn't you, then it must have been the person destroying our habitats!" Mindy exclaims.

"But how do we figure out who they are?" I say.

Just then I hear a rustle and a muffled thump. A shadowy figure emerges suddenly from behind the lifeguard's hut and starts running away!

"It's them!" I shout.

"Quick, we can catch them!" Mindy shouts.

But we all try to get up in a scramble of arms and legs and I fall back down, taking Mr Coast, Granny Jas and Mindy with me!

When I look up, the figure has gone. It's starting to get dark and there are very few street lights. We'll never be able to see which way they went. I notice a light flicker by the path that goes to the Dorm, but it goes out as quickly as it went on. They've gone.

"Let's check on our habitat and look around and see if they left anything behind. You never know!"

We all look around while Granny points the torch for us.

Quite quickly I find something! "Look." I point to a spade sticking out of the ground right next to our covered-over habitats. It looks like whoever had the spade was about to use it to destroy our work again! We must have frightened them off before they could start.

"That does look like sabotage! But the spade could belong to anyone," Mr Coast says.

I walk over to the spade to see if there's anything that could help our investigation, and spot a label attached! "Property of M.O.P.," I read aloud.

"Who's mop?" Granny asks.

"Not mop, M.O.P.," I say excitedly. "They're initials. I have a feeling that if we find M.O.P., then we'll find our culprit."

"Well, there aren't that many people in this town, it shouldn't be too difficult," Mr Coast says, picking up the spade. "Come on, you three, let's go and get some hot chocolate and the phone book, and we'll see what we can find out!"

"Thanks, Mr Coast," I say gratefully, as we walk back to the Dorm. "I know we sort of ambushed you back there **AND** accused you of destroying our project, but we are sorry about that and we do appreciate your help. And your sandcastles are **amazing!**"

Mr Coast chuckles. "That's alright, and you know what, I'm sort of glad someone knows my secret. Although I would prefer if you didn't tell anyone else. The locals will make such a fuss and I think I will tell them at some point, just not yet. Livvy doesn't know either. It's complicated, so please just keep it to yourselves for now?"

"We won't say anything," Mindy, Granny and I agree solemnly.

CHAPTER TEN

WHO IS M.O.P.?

We get back to the Dorm and Mr Coast says we can go and sit in his office while he gets the hot chocolate. While he's gone, we try to shake the sand off and tidy ourselves up a bit.

"Mop... Who could be Mop?" Granny asks, rubbing her chin.

"Shh, not so loud, Granny – and it's not Mop! **M dot O dot P dot**," I correct her.

Mr Coast comes back with a tray of hot chocolates, a plate of biscuits and the phone book. Behind him are Manny and Milo.

"I thought you might want your friends' help,"

Mr Coast says. "Don't worry, I was discreet – I just said I needed a hand putting out the bins."

"What happened to you three?" Milo asks, pointing at Granny, who is still shaking sand out of her sari.

"Long story!" I say. "But we found a clue. We saw the person who has been ruining our project. And they left this spade behind. It has initials on it, see? We just need to figure out what they stand for."

"Is that to help us?" Manny asks, pointing to the big yellow book Mr Coast is holding.

"It's a phone directory," Mr Coast explains. "It gives us the name and contact details for everyone who lives in the town. Well, everyone who has given permission for their details to be shared."

"I can probably find all that information on the internet," Manny says. "It would be quicker too."

"Er, nothing wrong with the good old-fashioned way." Mr Coast frowns.

"Let's see who's quickest then!" Manny challenges.

Milo jumps up. "I'll time you both!"

"Wait, what are we looking for?" Manny asks.

"We need to find someone in the town who has the initials M.O.P.," Mr Coast explains.

"So, a last name beginning with P. Okay, I guarantee I can do this faster than any crusty old phone book," Manny says, certain of himself.

Mr Coast smiles. "You're on! I'm up for a challenge." He beams more widely than I've seen since we met him.

"Is this a serious investigation or a competition?" I ask, but no one listens.

Mindy laughs. "Leave them to it, Anisha. Let's enjoy our hot chocolate."

So we sit back, sipping our drinks and watching Mr Coast flicking furiously through the phone directory and Manny tapping away on the computer.

Suddenly Manny raises his hand. "Got it."

Mr Coast looks up in despair. "Already?"

"What have you got?" I ask.

Manny shows me his screen. **"M.O.P. - Mike Oakley-Pearson!"**

"He's a very important police officer!" Mr Coast laughs. "Unlikely!"

Manny frowns and starts tapping away again. "Okay, how about Maud Patterson?"

"Dear old Maud runs the local Post Office. I can't imagine she has time for sabotage – plus she's almost ninety. I doubt she'd be running around in the dark on the beach!" Mr Coast scoffs.

"This is hopeless. There are no other M.O.P.s on here," Manny complains.

"Well, you're right about that. Nothing in here either," Mr Coast says.

A thought suddenly occurs to me. "What if M.O.P. isn't a local person?"

"Are you saying what I think you're saying?" Mindy asks.

"Yeah, what if M.O.P. is one of us, someone from our school! They wouldn't be in that directory of local people then, would they?"

"But why would someone from our school destroy our own project?" Mindy asks.

"Who knows, we've seen stranger things than this happen though!" I remind her, thinking of the spooky disco last term.

"That's actually true. Okay, whose name begins with M?" Milo asks.

"Well, yours," I say with a smile.

"And mine and Mindy's." Manny grins.

"It wasn't us! Was it?" Milo asks.

"No, of course it wasn't!" Mindy laughs.

"Who else?" I ask.

"Miriam?" Mindy suggests.

Granny snorts. "That quiet girl in the room next to yours? Never!"

"I have to agree with Granny," I reply. "Miriam's scared of everything, and I can't see her putting this whole sabotage plan together."

"Max from the other class?" Manny says.

"Maybe," says Mindy. "He's been quite homesick since we got here. I heard Miss Bunsen talking about it earlier. Would he sabotage the whole project, hoping we'd go home early?"

"Nah, I can't see it," I say. "And we saw him at lunch, so he can't have been down at the beach destroying everything."

"Who else then? I don't think there's anyone else whose name begins with M."

Granny leans forward in her chair. "You've forgotten someone. Actually, you probably wouldn't know them by their first name."

I look at Granny inquisitively, and then I realize what she's saying. It's a teacher! We only know teachers by their last names. My mind races. Which teacher has a surname beginning with P?

"Miss Poles – what's her full name?" I ask excitedly.

Granny grins triumphantly. **"It's Megan Poles!"**

"**Megan Poles, M.O.P!** Her middle name must be something beginning with O. It's her! Would she really do that, though? She was encouraging us."

"Why would she want to sabotage our project, Neesh?" Milo asks, looking hurt. "I thought she was a nice teacher. I thought she liked us."

"I don't know, Milo, but she has been behaving a bit oddly. This morning she said she went for a run in the blustery wind and she came back looking really dishevelled and distracted. But when we went out it wasn't that windy. Then when we realized all our habitat materials had gone missing, she didn't seem that concerned. It was just a bit weird. She keeps wandering off. She doesn't actually seem that bothered if we finish the habitat or not. But maybe she just has other important things on her mind."

"She mentioned her research," Mindy replies.

"Yeah, she was telling me about it," Milo adds. "She was saying she really hopes she gets her funding, because otherwise she won't be able to finish her research."

"But she's a teacher," Manny says. "She has a job. Why does she need to study?"

"Sometimes grown-ups keep studying," Granny explains. "They might just want to keep learning. You're never too old to learn something new, **beta**. But studying might also help a person get a different job or a better-paid job. I once thought about studying, you know. I wanted to be a pilot."

"What happened?" I ask.

"They weren't ready for me." Granny huffs. "Their loss!"

"Okay then," Mindy says, raising an eyebrow at me.

I clear my throat. "Anyway, so we think Miss Poles definitely had the opportunity to ruin the habitat. That could be her spade with the initials on it, and she's been acting a bit shady. Her motive is unclear, but it may be something to do with her research. Where was she when we were at lunch?"

"She was with you children," Granny says. "Just me and Miss Bunsen stayed behind to keep an eye on the habitats, remember!"

"Not the whole time," I say. "When we were having lunch, she went up to her room for a bit, or so she said. We were busy calling home from Mr Coast's office."

"Oh, were you now?" Mr Coast says, looking at us over his glasses.

I can feel a blush creep into my cheeks. Milo stares at the floor and Manny bites his lip.

"We're sorry, we know we shouldn't have," Mindy explains. "We were just really missing home, and our stepmum is about to have a baby. Our baby brother or sister."

Mr Coast smiles. "Well, I guess you have special circumstances. Just don't do it again without asking, okay?"

Mindy and Manny nod.

"Okay, so how long was Miss Poles gone for?" Granny asks.

"About thirty minutes. Enough time to run down

to the beach and ruin the habitat. I think she waited for Miss Bunsen and Granny to be distracted and she used that opportunity to wreck it."

"That's horrible," Granny says. "To think I offered that woman my special biriyani recipe!"

"Well, we know now, Granny. We just have to prove it's her," I say.

"Proof schmoof," Granny Jas yells. "I say we confront her now. Nobody can lie to Granny!"

"Granny, we can't just accuse a teacher like that!" I say. "We need to have hard evidence."

Granny sits back. "Okay, **beta**, we do it your way. What's the plan?"

CHAPTER ELEVEN

OMG, COULD IT BE....?

When we leave the office, all I can think is: how could she? I really liked Miss Poles. It's hard to believe she would go to such lengths to sabotage our project. The project she set for us! It doesn't make any sense. But the evidence seems to say she could be the one.

I toss and turn all night thinking about it, and just as I'm getting to sleep it's time to wake up.

"What's the plan today?" Mindy asks, as we stretch in our beds.

"I have no idea," I say. "We don't have quite enough evidence to confront Miss Poles yet. It's the last day of Beach Warriors, so if she really wants to ruin the competition then she'll have to make a move today. I guess we watch her carefully and be ready. Maybe we split into two teams. Manny and Milo can watch the habitats and make sure nothing else happens to them, and we'll watch Miss Poles."

"Okay, on it," Manny says, when we tell the boys the plan at breakfast.

"We can be like spies!" Milo adds.

"In disguise!" Manny finishes.

"I don't think you need disguises," I say, but it's too late, they're already talking about which costumes would help them go unnoticed best.

I see Miss Poles go past the dining room.

She's got her coat on. We have to follow her!

I pull Mindy along with me and signal to her to be quiet. Miss Poles is not going through the front door, though. She's using the side door – the one that leads to the path! Granny Jas passes us, so I grab her too. We might need reinforcements!

We follow at a distance and walk along the side of the building and towards the path, but there's no sign of Miss Poles. She must be walking quickly. We haven't gone far when I hear a noise behind us: the sound of shoes clicking on the path.

I stop walking and the noise stops.

"You okay?" Mindy asks. "Why did you stop?"

"I thought I heard something," I reply.

"It was probably just our own footsteps, **beta**," Granny says.

We carry on walking but there's that noise again. I turn back quickly to face whoever is following us – but there's no one there. But suddenly Miss Poles jumps out from behind a bush!

"Aha!" I shout. "We caught you!" I'm trying to sound confident but I'm shaking.

Miss Poles narrows her eyes at me. "What are you all doing? Were you following me? Why are you out here?"

"Why are **YOU** out here?" I reply.

"I don't think I like your tone!" Miss Poles says.

"The jig is up, Miss Poles. Or should we call you Mop!" Granny Jas says.

"Mop? What does that mean?" Miss Poles asks.

"M.O.P.," I say. "Your initials. We know it's you who's been sabotaging our project."

"Why on earth would I do that?" Miss Poles asks. She looks confused. I start to feel a sliver of doubt creep into my mind.

"Because you wanted to focus on your research and get your funding." Even as I say it, I know my reasoning doesn't sound right.

"That doesn't even make sense. It would make me a terrible teacher and a terrible person, plus it has no effect on whether I get funding or not anyway," Miss Poles argues. "And by the way, my initials do **NOT** spell out 'mop'! My middle name is Louise! So, do you want to tell me now what you're doing out here?"

I look at Mindy and Granny. "So, the spade we found last night isn't yours?" I ask.

Miss Poles sighs. "Well, no. What is going on?" So then I have to sheepishly explain our theory about the sabotage, and the clues that led us here.

Miss Poles, thankfully, has a sense of humour. "I can't believe you thought I'd ruin your project! But I do see how my behaviour might have seemed a little scatty. I knew we weren't supposed to be taking phone calls but I was expecting important news, and so that's why I kept wandering off! I was trying to find a phone signal – it's a nightmare here on the coast!"

"Oh," I say, disappointed. I really thought we had it sussed this time.

"Oh dear. It seems we have accused you wrongly, **beta**," Granny says. "Sorry!"

"That's okay. Are you out here investigating then? Maybe I can help," Miss Poles offers.

"I don't know how," I say glumly. "I keep thinking I've figured it out and then I accuse the wrong person!"

Miss Poles smiles kindly. "Anisha, you're a scientist. You know we have to experiment many times before we hit on the right solution to a problem. You just haven't found it yet."

"Thanks, miss," I say gratefully. "I guess I'm just really upset more for Milo. He's so sad about his nan's birdbath, and I just don't understand why someone is trying so hard to ruin our project."

"I don't really understand it either, Anisha, but look, there are plenty of us and maybe we can put our heads together and come up with some ideas. We might even find that birdbath yet," Miss Poles says.

I feel a bit better then. "I'm sorry I accused you," I say. I pull out my map and stare at it. I have no clue what to do now!

"What's that?" Miss Poles asks.

"Oh, it's just an idea I had about how the culprit ran on and off the beach, and where they might have hidden," I say. "Mr Graft said there might be caves

along this bit here. We were going to try and find them."

"And did you?" Miss Poles asks.

I hit my hand to my forehead. "No! We were going to, then we didn't and I completely forgot about it! We need to go and check the caves – there might be a clue!" I say.

Granny grins at both of us. "Well, what are we waiting for? Let's go!"

CHAPTER TWELVE

A CLUE IN THE CAVE!

We walk down the path in a single-file line. Me at the front, then Mindy, then Granny and finally Miss Poles at the back. When we reach the beach we go to the right, towards the shoreline over to where Mr Graft said the caves might be.

There's a big wall of rocks; I can't see any caves though.

"There's nothing here." I wave my arms around, feeling frustrated.

"Wait, what's that?" Mindy shouts, pointing behind me.

I look around, and it's not obvious but there's

definitely a gap in the rocks. We run over to see, and it is – it's a cave!

Mindy grabs my hand. "Wait, there could be a bear or something in there!"

"It's unlikely that a bear would be this close to the sea," Miss Poles says. "Don't worry, I'll go first."

We tread carefully. It's dark in the cave, so Granny turns her torch on. I feel something under my foot.

"Granny, point the torch here, please?"

"What is it, **beta**? Oh look, it's only a piece of paper."

"It's got something written on it, look," Mindy says.

She's right, the word *Ideas* is at the top of the crumpled paper, and then under that, *Community Beach Clean*.

"Okay, that's weird. I doubt many people come down here, and there doesn't seem to be any other rubbish on the floor. I wonder who wrote this?" I say. "There might be more clues in the cave. We should go in."

"No way," says Mindy.

"We have to if we want to solve this mystery," I say firmly.

"I'm here, **beta**, no one will mess with us, okay?" Granny Jas assures us.

"Hmm. Should we go and get Mr Graft first?" Miss Poles worries. "I'm just not sure about this."

But I'm already halfway into the cave, there's no turning back now. "I need to know who is behind everything that's happened. Milo's birdbath could be here for all we know!" I say as I move forward into the cave.

"Caves are creepy." Mindy shivers. "I don't like this at all. I just want to make that clear right now!"

A strange flapping sound echoes around us. "You don't think there are bats in here, do you?" Mindy asks.

"Shh," I say. "I don't think there are any bats. Probably not, anyway."

"That's not very reassuring, Anisha," Mindy says, grabbing my hand again. "Stay close."

We step forward slowly. Granny offers to sing a song to help us not be scared, but before she can start, her light lands on something on the floor in the corner of the cave. It's covered in a cloth. My hand shakes as I reach out to pull the cloth off. I lift it up and Granny shines the light on it. It's a blazer!

"Woah!" Mindy exclaims. "Wait, a blazer?"

"Let's head back and we can look at it properly in the light," Miss Poles suggests.

We go outside into the daylight and I look more closely at the blazer. There's a name label, but it's way too worn and faded to read. I turn it the right way and see there's a badge on it.

It's an orange and green emblem, like the one we have on our school uniform but different, and underneath the logo it has the initials M.O.P.

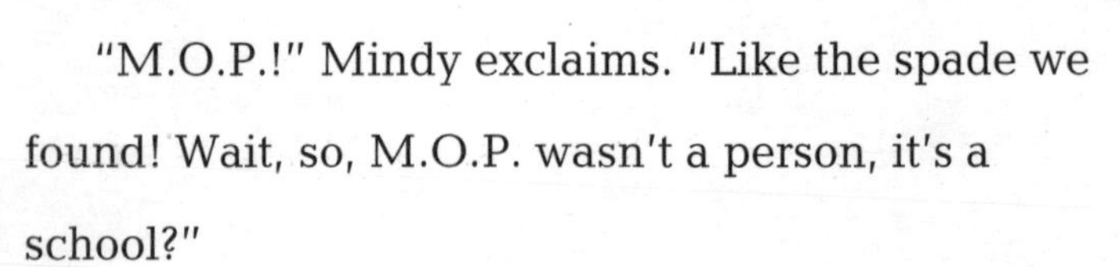

"M.O.P.!" Mindy exclaims. "Like the spade we found! Wait, so, M.O.P. wasn't a person, it's a school?"

"Remember what Beena said about the person who knocked into her, carrying a blazer?" I say. "This must be where they've been hiding, in between sabotaging our project!"

Miss Poles jumps up and down. "I know what M.O.P. stands for!"

"You do? How?" I ask.

"When I signed us up for Beach Warriors, there were other schools on the list already. M.O.P. was one of them. Morley Oaks Primary School," Miss Poles says proudly.

"They must have sabotaged our habitats because they want to win Beach Warriors for themselves!" I say.

"So how do we figure out who from there it is?" Mindy asks.

"We'll interrogate them all!" Granny Jas yells, waggling her finger.

"I don't think that'll be necessary," I say. "I have an idea."

I look again at the piece of paper we found earlier. "It says 'Ideas: Community Beach Clean'. This looks like a list of ideas of projects for Beach Warriors. It must have been written by somebody who goes to

M.O.P. Only it looks like they gave up on their own project and decided to ruin ours instead. Whoever wrote this is the person we're looking for."

"It's just a list though, Anisha. Anyone from the school could have written it," Mindy points out.

"I think I have a way of narrowing it down," I say, looking closely at the handwriting on the piece of paper. "Look at the way this person curls their letter C. How many people do that? I feel like I've seen this writing somewhere before... I just need to remember where!"

I sit down on a rock, with a million thoughts racing through my head. Blazers, handwriting, local kids... There must be some clue we're missing?

Miss Poles asks out loud what we're all wondering: "What do we do now?"

Then a memory pops into my head. "I didn't think much of it at the time, but...Mindy, remember those boys on the bikes we met on the way to the caves? They weren't very welcoming at all, talking about how the beach should be left to locals. Maybe it was them. They didn't want visitors to win the competition," I say. "The 'Go Away' message on the beach would fit with them too."

"Oh yeah, Danny and William!" Mindy remembers.

"But how would we prove they had anything to do with what's been going on, **beta**? Do you want me to have a word with them?" Granny asks.

"No, calm down, we can't just go accusing them," I say. "We need to think about this. Let's go back and get some breakfast and rejoin the group, otherwise everyone is going to wonder where we've got to."

We walk back to the Dorm pretty much in silence. I know what we're all thinking: today is the last day of the project and then we go home. The whole trip has been a disaster; nothing has gone to plan.

We have hardly any time to finish our habitats before the Beach Warriors deadline at four o'clock, no idea who it is that's out to get us and we still haven't any idea how to find Milo's birdbath!

At breakfast we catch Milo and Manny up, and they're just as downhearted as us. Afterwards though, when we're walking back down to the beach, Granny decides we've spent long enough feeling down and declares, "I've had a brilliant idea!"

"We were just going to—" I start to say.

"No time for that, we're going to play kabaddi!* It is the perfect activity to cheer everyone up, and it will be a good distraction!" Granny grins.

"Oh no, please not kabaddi, Granny. You know I'm rubbish at it," I say.

*** Kabaddi is a contact team sport played between two teams of seven players. Granny says it's such an old game it used to be played by people in Ancient Indian times! I wonder if they were as bad at it as me?!**

"Kabaddi, is it that game Dad watches?" Mindy asks Manny.

"Yeah, the one they play in India. It's like tag but not really," Manny says.

"It's a very complex and competitive sport played not just in India." Granny huffs. "Come on, I'll show you. It's going to be fun!"

"But we haven't got much time left to finish our project, there's so much to do!" I say.

"Half an hour, that's all I ask. Everyone needs a lift, beta, enough of this down in the dumpers, okay? We're going to put a smile on all these sad faces," Granny says, determined.

And she's not messing about, within a few moments she's convinced the teachers and some local kids to join in too. She tries to get a few random parents involved, but they're not having it at all.

Milo nudges me. "Look, Neesh, it's those boys!"

I look, and it's Danny and William! This is our chance.

"Come on, I think I have an idea," I say.

"What are we doing?" Milo asks.

"We're going to play kabaddi!" I grin. "And while we're doing that, we're going to get some proof that either William or Danny left their blazer and that list in the cave."

"How?" Mindy asks.

"Just follow my lead," I say.

Granny gathers everyone in a circle. "Right, we split into two teams. Each team has a player called the raider. The object of this game is for them to infiltrate the other side and tag as many of their team as possible – while avoiding being tackled themselves – and return to their own side safely. Anyone who is not the raider has to try to tackle the raider of the other team and not get tagged themselves. Got it?"

Everyone shakes their heads, so Granny explains it again and demonstrates a tackle on Mr Graft, which is quite funny. Eventually we get started.

We split into the two teams. Mindy, Manny, Milo and I offer to be with the local kids, Team A. I make sure I position myself near to Danny; he looks like the less scary one of the two.

Granny pulls out a whistle from her bag (she really does have everything in there!) and declares herself referee.

"When I blow the whistle, Team A" – she points to us – "you pick one person to be your raider. They have to go forward past this line and try to tag one of the other team's players. Team B, if you can reach forward and tag the raider without being tagged yourself, then you can get them out! Who wants to be a raider first?"

Everyone steps back except Mindy, who smiles shyly and puts her hand up. "I'll have a go," she says.

"Good for you, Mindy **beta**!" Granny cheers. "Right, are we ready?" And with that, Granny blows on the whistle.

Mindy runs forward super fast. The other team aren't ready and she manages to tag the player on the end really quickly and then run away so they can't get her. We all cheer. Mindy looks like she's surprised herself, and then she grins at us and jumps up and down.

Granny shouts, "One point to Team A!"

Then Mindy goes again. This time she does a fake-out move where she acts like she's going one way but then goes another. We're all shouting her name by this point. I don't normally enjoy sports, but it's so fun watching Mindy!

On the third try Beena manages to get Mindy out, but only by some weird accident where she slips on the sand and tags Mindy with her foot. Mindy is well annoyed.

After a few turns on each side, it's my go as raider. My tummy does somersaults. I'm so not good at sports. I run forward when Granny blows the whistle, but I catch my foot on a rock and go flying into the line of people on the other team, taking them and myself out. Everyone is really nice and tries to make me feel okay about it, but I think I'm better off on the sideline!

Team B turn out to be quite good, but we manage to hold our own and we get the chance to revive a player. We pick Mindy of course and she goes back out to big cheers.

After a little while Danny gets taken out too. I take the opportunity to go and sit next to him.

"So, who would have thought we'd be on the same team!" I say brightly.

"Yeah, I guess." He shrugs.

"I mean, I feel like we got off on the wrong foot. We weren't trying to make enemies," I offer.

"Enemies? That's a bit extreme. We hardly know you!" Danny says.

"Yeah, but you were all super annoyed we were on your beach and taking part in the competition. Isn't that why you hate us?"

"Well, we definitely don't hate you, and to be honest we weren't that fussed about the competition," Danny confesses.

"We thought you hated us **BECAUSE** of the competition!" I say.

Danny laughs nervously. "Well, I guess we were a little mean. We just get a bit protective of Coral Cove – lots of people come here on trips, and not everyone respects the beach and where we live, or understands it's our home. But we've seen you cleaning up the beach, so I'm sorry we were so suspicious. And this game, kabaddi, is really fun! I've not played a big game like this on the beach with strangers before."

"I guess I can understand that," I reply.

"Actually to be honest there was only one person in our whole year who was even interested in the beach project competition. Most people were going away for the holiday or had other things to do."

"The person who cared about doing the project in your year. Who was it?" I ask excitedly.

"Oh, you might have met her actually," Danny replies. "Her dad runs the Dorm!"

"Livvy?" I say, confused. "She didn't seem that bothered to me."

"Well, in school she was making a right fuss. Saying it's our beach and we should be

representing the area in the competition, and it's only right the beach is named after the people that live here," Danny tells me.

"Oh," I say, my heart sinking. Livvy was so friendly to us.

I never imagined it could be her. She was offering to help us. It doesn't make sense, and yet in my heart I know it now. It's been Livvy sabotaging us this whole time.

Granny blows the whistle, because the last person has been tagged and the match is over.

"Team B win!" she declares, holding up Miss Bunsen's arm. Miss Bunsen looks red in the face from running, but as pleased as I've ever seen her. My team look exhausted but happy, even though we didn't win.

Danny goes to be with his friends and Mindy, Manny and Milo flop onto the sand next to me. "That looked like an interesting conversation," Mindy says.

"Yeah, I learned quite a lot. I think maybe we judged Danny and William too quickly," I say. "But Danny just told me something. I think I know who actually did it now! But you won't like it..."

CHAPTER THIRTEEN

WHO REALLY DID IT!

When I've finished speaking, everyone just sits gawping at me.

"How? Why? Are you sure it was Livvy?" Mindy asks.

"I know, I know – and I wish so much that I was wrong!" I say. "But the evidence leads to her. Danny said only one person in their year at M.O.P. was really bothered that they weren't taking part in the beach competition. That person was Livvy."

"Okay, so she really wanted to be part of the competition. How do we prove she was so against us winning that she sabotaged us, three times?" Mindy asks.

"And took my nan's birdbath!" Milo adds.

"I have an idea," I say. "It's a long shot, but do you remember the piece of paper we found in the cave with the blazer..."

"The list of competition ideas?" Milo says.

"Yes. This list," I say, pulling it out of my pocket. "Look at the way the letter C is curled round. If Livvy writes her Cs like that, she must be the culprit."

"Okay, we'd need Livvy to write something down for us so we can compare handwriting. How do we get her to do that?" Manny asks.

"We don't need to. I already know where we can get a sample of her handwriting," I say. "I saw it the other day when we were in Mr Coast's office. I just need to go back and get it."

"And then what? Do we confront her?" Milo asks.

"I don't know yet," I say. "We also still need to figure out how we're going to finish our habitats by the deadline today, without her ruining it again."

Suddenly Milo jumps up. "Oh no!" he yelps, and he runs off to a mound of sand nearby.

I chase after him, watching him kneel down to pick something up. "What is it, Milo?"

As I get closer, I can see he's holding a seagull!

"Milo, those things are flying rats!" Mindy squeals, running up behind us. "They carry diseases and they steal your food and they're just nasty!"

"Seagulls aren't nasty, don't say that!" Milo says. "Anyway, this one's hurt, look. I saw it was limping. Its foot is caught in some plastic. Help me get it off."

"I'm not touching it!" Mindy shouts and runs off.

"Neesh, will you help me?" Milo asks. "I can't just leave him like this."

I don't like seagulls any more than Mindy, but Milo is my best friend, so of course when he asks me to help him I have to.

"What do I need to do?" I ask.

"I'll hold him. Just gently pull that bit of plastic around and off his foot."

Milo holds the seagull carefully in both hands, keeping it secure and calm by talking gently to it. The seagull seems to quite like him, as it turns its head to one side like it's listening to him. I lean forward.

"Okay, I'm doing it, I'm doing it, I'm doing it," I squeal as I gently pull the plastic off the seagull's foot.

"This is why people shouldn't leave their rubbish on the beach – it's so harmful to the wildlife," Milo says sadly.

Milo checks the seagull's foot and thankfully

there are no cuts. He places the seagull gently down on the ground and says, "There you go, Siva."

"Siva? Where did you get that name from?" I ask.

"One of Granny Jas's programmes that she watches. Sometimes when you're busy with other stuff I sit and watch them with her," Milo says.

"How did I not know this?" I laugh.

Siva the seagull looks at Milo for a moment and then waddles away.

"Come back soon!" Milo calls out. "You're welcome at my habitat anytime!" He adds sadly, "He'd have loved the birdbath."

"He'll still love your habitat," I say, patting Milo on the arm.

"If we ever manage to finish building them," Manny says. "I'm not sure we have enough time. We should have been putting the finishing touches on now and there's still so much to do!"

"We'll figure it out," I say. "We're a good team, we can do anything."

Suddenly it comes to me. "I know!" I shout, standing up. "Everyone, listen up. I know how we can still finish on time to take part in Beach Warriors.

"We are a **GREAT** team, so why not use that, our great teamwork! We can all work together! Milo was working on a habitat that had different levels for different creatures. What if we build on that and put **ALL** our ideas together in one big super habitat? A habitat that welcomes all wildlife! Lots of levels and different areas. Feeders for the different creatures. Obviously we'll keep the predators in a separate area so they're not tempted to eat their friends! Ooh and a rock pool for the water-based wildlife. What do you think?"

Milo beams. "I love that. It's like my idea but super-sized!"

"That sounds awesome!" Manny agrees.

Mindy nudges me. "You always have the best ideas." She smiles.

I shrug. "It's Milo's idea really, I just made it bigger."

"Take some credit for once!" Mindy scolds me. "You are awesome, Anisha."

We explain our idea to Miss Poles, and then Milo and I get to brief everyone on what the new plan for the habitat is. Just as we're about to start building again, Livvy comes to join us.

"I missed you guys at breakfast!" She smiles.

"Oh, we just popped out early for some air." I smile back, hoping my face doesn't give away that I know what she's done.

"I can help this morning, just show me what to do," Livvy says. "I did all my fractions super quick so I could be free to spend some time at the beach with you all!"

"That's really great," I reply, thinking it might be the chance I need.

Beena comes over then, smiling broadly at us, which is weird right away. "Right, team, I've made up a schedule for everyone. We don't have a minute to lose today! Now that we're making a super habitat, everything must be planned and executed to the **MINUTE!**" With that, she flings a pile of papers at us and walks off.

"What's that all about?" Livvy asks.

"We came up with a plan for a super habitat to combine all our ideas and save time," I explain. "Beena has somehow put herself in charge and is telling everyone what to do. For some reason she's suddenly got into the spirit of the project and now she wants to help. Well, this **IS** Beena, so her idea of helping is actually more like telling everyone where to be and what to do. I think she's taken on the role of site manager! She did ask Mr Graft for a hard hat, but he gave her a withering look and that was the end of that."

"I don't see her digging up any sand or doing any actual work though," Mindy grumbles.

"It's quite genius actually," Manny comments. "She looks busy but she's making us do all the work!"

"This schedule looks complicated," Milo groans. "What are all these boxes?"

"Time slots, I think," I say, as we all peer at the piece of paper. It's a spreadsheet. Dad has them for work sometimes. But this one has a timeline running across the top and then columns for each part of the habitat. Beena has used a different colour for each column and she's used glitter pens to write the names. It's **A LOT**, and my eyes hurt just looking at it.

"Wow," Livvy says, squinting at it.

"Yeah, wow!" Mindy says, laughing, but she's looking at me like, *What now?*

We quickly start work on the super habitat, using the materials from yesterday and making new bits when we need to. We've even come up with a name for it: **SANDY TOWERS!** You won't believe it, but it was Beena's idea!

Mr Graft draws out the space on the sand with a big stick, and Miss Bunsen makes piles of the different building materials with some of the group, so we can make the different areas of the habitat.

Livvy makes a big show of helping, but I see her eyeing our pile of materials.

"What can we do to help?" Mindy asks me.

"I've had an idea. Can you can keep Livvy occupied while I go and find the piece of paper in her dad's office?" I say, nodding towards Livvy.

"We're on it," Mindy says.

"Wait – I can't be nice to her, knowing what I know now!" Milo protests. "I'll just end up giving us away!"

"Okay, you come with me then," I say.

"What do we say to her about where you've gone?" Manny panics. "I'm not good at lying!"

"Breathe, Manny!" Mindy instructs him. "Just nod and agree with whatever I say, okay?"

Manny nods.

"Will you be okay?" I ask. "Just distract her with the super habitat. You'll be great!"

"We'll be fine," Mindy reassures me. "I'm just going to say that miss sent you to get some stuff from the Dorm and you'll be back in a bit."

I give them a thumbs up, give a big fake smiley wave to Livvy and Milo, and Manny and I go off in the opposite direction.

We run up the beach and straight into the Dorm.

It's empty and the door to Mr Coast's office is open. I run in and look around. Where was it?

"There, that piece of paper!" I say, pointing by Milo's head.

It's a note from Livvy to her dad saying, *Don't forget to get more cheese and crackers!*. In curly writing.

My heart dips.

So it is true. It makes me a little sad to know for definite.

"The Cs, they're just like the ones on the piece of paper from the cave!" Milo exclaims.

"Exactly," I say, putting the note in my pocket. "Come on, we need to get this back to the beach."

We race back and see our group has made great progress with the super habitat. It's really taking shape and everyone is buzzing about busily.

Mindy spots us and scoots over. "Did you get it?" she breathes.

"Yeah, and it proves what we thought. How has everything been here?" I ask, smiling at Livvy, who is walking across to us now.

"Fine. She's been asking lots of questions about the build, though. I think I managed to sound normal and calm about everything."

"Well done. We only have to keep it up for a bit longer. I have a plan. Just agree with what I say, okay?"

"We've got your back, Neesh," Milo says.

"Hey, all okay, Anisha?" Livvy asks. "These guys said you went to get some stuff from the Dorm. Did you bring it?" She looks at our empty hands.

"Oh, er, we realized we didn't need it." I laugh. "Wasted trip, but at least we got our exercise in for today!"

"Ha, well I think we're breaking for lunch soon. I'd better go back and help Dad." Livvy smiles.

"I had fun, though, thanks for letting me help out."

"No worries!" I say, quickly thinking of a plan. "Were you thinking of coming back later, Livvy? I don't think we'll be here till about two o'clock, because Miss Bunsen was saying she wanted us to do some writing up or something first."

Livvy's eyes flash. "Oh, really? Okay, well I have stuff to do this afternoon anyway, so I might just see you at dinner time back at the Dorm then," she says.

Once Livvy is gone, Mindy turns to me. "What was that about?"

"All part of the plan," I explain. "If Livvy thinks we won't be here until two, she'll think she has time to come back and sabotage Sandy Towers."

"But we won't really be at lunch?" Milo asks. "Because I am kind of peckish."

"No, Milo, we can just grab a snack – we have important work to do to get ready for when Livvy comes back! We're going to set a **TRAP**!"

CHAPTER FOURTEEN

THE TRAP

A little while later, we get Granny to cover for us when everyone in our group has gone back to the Dorm for lunch. Mindy, Manny, Milo and I set to work. It doesn't take long to build the trap once we get to grips with what we're doing. I got the idea from a science programme I watched on the kids channel at home. Except the one they made on there was much smaller. There is a slightly unfortunate incident when Manny steps onto the plank which we have balanced on top of an old beach ball. Mindy is kneeling at the other end and the plank swings upwards and hits her from behind. She is not happy!

We dig a hole to support the beach ball and then another hole under one end of the plank so that when someone steps on it, the other end swings up like a see-saw, flinging seaweed all over them. We cover the whole thing in twigs and more seaweed so it doesn't look obvious at all.

"Are you sure it will work?" Mindy asks.

"Yes, pretty sure anyway," I say. "Positioning is everything."

Milo nudges me. "It's lucky Mr Coast had that stuff in the Dorm shed. Can we test it?"

"There's no time," I say. "We just have to hope it works."

"Oh man, I really want to go and jump on it now," Manny says.

"No – if you do that it'll go off, and then we'll have to reset the whole trap!" I say.

I see movement at the top of the beach. It's Livvy, and she's coming this way!

"Duck down!" I whisper as we all hide behind a rock.

Livvy is holding a broom and marching towards our super habitat. I can't believe she really means to destroy Sandy Towers, after all our hard work!

"Wait for it," I whisper. "Any second now."

Livvy goes to swing the broom at our habitat!

As she does, she places her foot down on the plank and I can tell from her face that she realizes something isn't right. She looks down, and the other end of the plank swings up and the seaweed comes flying over, covering Livvy!

That's when our group and teachers come back from lunch.

Mindy, Manny, Milo and I run up front, and everyone else follows us.

Miss Bunsen tries to ask what's going on, but she gets pushed to the side by the rush of children.

"It **WAS** you!" I gasp at Livvy.

"You used poor Mr Wriggles in your evil plan," cries Milo. "How could you frame a cat! And **WHERE** is my nan's birdbath?!"

Livvy brushes sloppy seaweed out of her face. "I've got the birdbath – it's safe, don't worry."

"Why did you do it?" I ask her. "I thought we were friends."

She looks sad for a second, then looks me right in the eye. "We were, it's just... People out of town always think they know what's best for us and our seaside. This is our town. It used to be such a happy place. Then, when the secret sandcastles started popping up, someone posted a picture of one online and suddenly we're a tourist spot!"

"Tourists are good for businesses, aren't they?" I ask quietly.

"That's not the point. This is my home. But now the beach I used to run up and down with my mum is overcrowded and dirty. When they announced that competition, it felt like an opportunity to reclaim it. But nobody at my school wanted to help me. And then you all turned up with your amazing habitats... It's like nothing is just ours any more."

She looks sad and angry, and I'm not sure what the right thing to say is, so I try, "I think I know what you mean."

"How can you?" Livvy scoffs.

"Well, I have been feeling like that a bit with my family," I say, trying not to look at Granny or Mindy and Manny.

"You have?" Livvy sniffs.

I reach out my hand to help her up off the ground. "Yeah. We have a new baby coming, home is always chaotic, and I guess I feel like nothing is just mine any more. I love my family, but I feel a bit

like I don't know where I fit in right now. There's so many of us, and I'm not the loudest one so I don't always feel like I'm being heard."

My face feels really hot as I admit this. I can feel Granny's eyes boring into me as I speak.

"Things were fine when my mum was here," Livvy says. "We were happy. I liked living in Coral Cove. It all changed after she left us and Dad stopped wanting to go to the beach. Then the tourists came, and it's never been the same. It was **OUR** beach."

"But why destroy our project over and over?" I ask. "How does that help any of what you're talking about?"

Livvy shrugs. "I was angry. I just wanted you all to go away and life to go back to how it was. I started off just scattering your rubbish and just in case you were suspicious I tried to throw you off by framing Mr Wriggles with his hairballs and paw prints.
I thought that would be enough to put you off, but

then you cleared it all up, and salvaged all those materials in your scavenger hunt. So I hid them, but you went and found them. I had no choice, so I wrecked what you built. I hoped you'd just give up after that."

"But didn't you think that by making all that mess and leaving all the litter across the beach, you were destroying the place you say you love?" I point out.

Livvy looks down at her feet. "I guess I didn't think it through. All I could think was that I didn't want you to win the competition. If you won, I knew you'd name the beach something like Birmingham Beach – but if we won, I wanted to name it after my mum. Maybe then she'd see it in the paper and come back to us."

I realize someone is behind me. It's Mr Coast, and he's been listening to everything.

"Oh, Livvy," he says. "Why didn't you talk to me?" He runs over and hugs her, but she pushes him away.

"You never want to talk about Mum or any of it!" Livvy shouts.

Mr Coast sighs. "I know, you're right. Listen, I'm here now and we can talk about anything you want."

"What's the point?" Livvy sighs. "Just ground me and be done with it."

"I'm not going to ground you, Livvy. You know why? Because then you won't be able to put all this right.

"Sweetheart, I don't think naming the beach after your mum would make her come back. I know that's hard, and we can talk about it anytime. I'm sorry I haven't been great at that. And if it's anyone's fault that Coral Cove got famous, it's mine. Blame me," Mr Coast says.

"You? Why?"

"Because, well...I'm the Secret Sand-Maker."

Livvy looks at him wide-eyed. "You are? It makes sense... Of course it's you!" She laughs. "So I've been mad about something that my own dad has been doing all this time?"

Mr Coast scratches his head. "Well, yeah, I guess so."

They both start laughing then.

"Look, it's not too late to make something positive out of all this," I say. "We could make your beach beautiful again. We can work together and make it the best it's ever been!"

"You mean it?" Livvy asks.

"Yes! We came here to do something positive, and that's what we're going to do," I say. "Let's make a plan."

As we gather everyone together, Granny takes me to one side.

"**Beta**, did you mean what you said? About not knowing where you fit in any more, and about it all being a lot with the baby coming?"

I nod silently.

"Oh, **beta**, you should have told me. I know we're all making a fuss right now, but that's just the excitement. Family life will soon settle down again. And as for your place in our family, don't you know you are the heart of it?"

I look at Granny, and my eyes feel all wet. "You really mean that?"

"Of course, **beta**. Why do you think I muscled my way on to this trip? If anything, I felt like you didn't really want me here!"

My cheeks feel hot, because I know Granny is right. "Well," I say slowly, "I guess I was annoyed at first. Even though I've been feeling left out, I was looking forward to being independent, and when you said you were coming on the trip it was a bit..." I try to find the right word.

Granny smiles. "Suffocating?"

"I mean, er, I wouldn't say that," I say. "But I could have done without you telling baby stories about me to everyone! I don't know, Granny. I just feel confused and a bit lost sometimes. There's always something going on in our family. There's never just a normal day."

"What is normal?" Granny asks. "Our normal is different to everyone else's. So what? But I understand – sometimes it would be nice to have some quiet time, right?"

I nod again. "I'm sorry I made you feel like I didn't want you here," I tell her. "I'm glad we're talking about it."

"I'm sorry I butted in where I wasn't needed," Granny says, hugging me. "I think I'm just scared you're getting so big now that you won't need me at all any more."

I laugh. "Granny, don't be silly! I will **ALWAYS** need you!"

We all sit down and put together a plan to make the beach the best it's ever been and bring the community together to raise awareness, like we'd hoped to do with our habitat. If this is going to work, we have to all pull together.

Livvy runs back to the Dorm with William and Danny, and they fill a trolley full of supplies and meet us back at the beach. She also brings Milo's nan's birdbath and gives it back to him.

"I am really sorry I took it," she tells him.

"It's okay. I'm just glad it's safe." Milo smiles.

Mindy smiles as we start drawing out a big sign that says **COMMUNITY BEACH CLEAN**. "This was a really nice idea, Anisha."

"I get why Livvy was so sad, and if we can make something good come out of all this then I'll be happy," I say. "It was never really about winning the competition. Which gives me an idea, well it was Livvy's idea actually… Tell me what you think!"

A little later, Livvy, William and Danny run round handing out the posters we've made, inviting all the local residents and business owners to come down to the beach. Within an hour, we have quite a crowd of people. We split off into groups, each covering different areas of the beach. Some work on the coastline and the shrubs and bushes, some rake the sand for smaller bits of rubbish, some check the shore for bits of plastic that have been swept out in the water and might harm the marine life.

Our group carry on putting the finishing touches to our super habitat – it doesn't take that long with everyone helping.

Livvy smiles as we stand back to admire it. "You'll definitely win the competition now!" she says.

"Oh, I should tell you – we decided to withdraw our habitat, Sandy Towers from the competition," I say. "It didn't feel right, once we knew what the beach means to you all. It should definitely be named by someone who lives here. But we had the idea earlier to make another entry as a collective, us teamed up with you all. The beach clean is our entry now, together. If we win, you get to name the beach!

The community beach clean was your original idea, after all – I found it on your planning list in the cave. Miss Poles agreed it's a great idea."

Livvy looks like she might cry. She hugs me tightly. "Anisha, you might be the nicest person I've ever met," she says.

We finish the habitat and take pictures with Mr Coast's old camera.

"Want to build a sandcastle to go next to it?" he asks Livvy with a smile.

"Really?" Livvy beams.

Mr Coast shows us how to shape the sand and put in the detail. We all make a castle – well, mine looks more like a block of flats – and it's like we've made a little community right there on the beach!

"We should have a pooja!" Granny exclaims. "In our culture we always bless a new home."

She's so excited, and everyone gathers round. Granny lights a diva she finds in her bag that always seems to have the right thing at the right time. She says a little prayer and sprinkles a few drops of water on Sandy Towers. For the first time, it feels nice to be part of a blessing.

Mindy squeezes my hand. "We did it, Anisha!"

"I know. I wasn't sure we'd be able to. And look, Livvy seems so much closer to her dad too. It's really nice," I say.

"I was thinking about what you said, Anisha; about the baby changing everything. You know how important you are to me, right?"

"Oh, er, yeah, I guess," I say, feeling super awkward.

"Anisha, you showed me how to be part of this family. It doesn't matter what happens now, you'll always be my best friend and cousin," Mindy says.

"I...I don't know what to say," I stumble. "I'm not good at this stuff."

"Ha, neither am I, remember?" Mindy laughs. "Come on, let's go and build some more sandcastles. We only have a few hours left here, before we have to head home – might as well make the most of it!"

Miss Poles runs back to the Dorm to submit our competition entry and all the photos we've taken. We won't find out till next week because the judges will have to look at all the entries carefully, but I really hope we win for Livvy. Even if we don't, I have a feeling she and her dad will be just fine. And after everything, we all kind of feel like winners anyway.

The sun comes out and it's turning into the nicest day. We have a couple of hours left and everyone is having a lovely time together. Somebody has brought sandwiches and crisps, and we all have a picnic right there on the beach. The woman from the ice-cream parlour brings us all cones and we sit by the shore letting the waves lap over our bare feet. Miss Bunsen hasn't quite conquered her fear of the water but she stands a bit closer to it than she has before and for once she doesn't look like she wants to run away!

Just as I'm feeling the most relaxed ever, Miss Poles comes running over.

"I just got a message on my laptop. It was delayed because of the signal here. You need to call home. Right now!"

CHAPTER FIFTEEN

A NEW ARRIVAL

Mindy, Manny, Milo and I race back up to the Dorm, where Mr Coast is sweeping outside on the front step.

"Where's the fire?" he jokes, but then he sees we're all panicked. "What is it?" he asks, looking concerned.

"We got a message to call home," I say. "It sounds urgent."

"Use my office," he says.

We run to Mr Coast's office and I dial my house on the phone. No answer.

"Try our house," Mindy suggests.

No answer there either.

"Dad's mobile!" Manny offers.

We dial the number, and I can feel we're all holding our breath. Granny has joined us now too and she places her hands on my shoulders. I'm thinking, *Please pick up. Please pick up the phone.*

"Hello?" It's Uncle Tony. I press the speakerphone button.

"Uncle Tony, it's me, Anisha. We just got your message. Is everyone okay? We tried my house and your house." I stumble over my words.

There's silence and then he says, "We're okay, Anisha. Are Mindy and Manny there?"

"We're here, Dad," they say at the same time. "Is Bindi there?"

"Er, well, she is, but… Here, let me put her on."

"Hello." Aunty Bindi sounds tired. I'm worried. I squeeze Mindy's hand.

"Are you okay?" Manny asks her.

"I'm okay," Bindi answers. "Just a bit worn out.

I have someone I want you to meet… Kids, meet baby Maya." And then we hear the most beautiful snuffly breathing.

"Is that…?" Mindy looks at me wide-eyed.

"Is that the baby? She came already?" Manny asks. His eyes are shining too.

Aunty Bindi laughs. "Yes! She's here and she's so beautiful. She has your hair, Manny, and your eyes, Mindy!"

We're all crying then and hugging. We think about doing a videocall, but then we decide we want to see baby Maya in person properly when we get home. It turns out that Aunty Bindi had the baby yesterday but didn't want to disturb our trip. They're coming home from the hospital later today, and I cannot wait!

And do you know the weirdest thing – all through the call, even though it was all about the baby, my tummy wasn't in knots even one little bit.

A few hours later, it's the evening and we're back home, waiting for Aunty Bindi and Uncle Tony to arrive. My tummy is full of butterflies, Mindy is pacing up and down and Manny can't sit still either.

Finally we hear a car pull up outside. It's them!

Before we can even get to the door, Granny Jas comes running through the house and gets there first!

"**BETA!** Oh, where is she, my little ladoo!"

"Let them in the door, Mum!" Dad tells her.

I stay sitting on the sofa while everyone buzzes around Aunty Bindi and Uncle Tony and the baby car seat they've brought into the house. Mindy holds

baby Maya first, and she looks so proud. Then Manny holds her and starts telling his new little sister all the things he's going to teach her, like survival and martial arts.

Everyone else has a turn holding the baby – it's such a happy moment, but I feel like I'm on the outside looking in. Then Aunty Bindi looks over at me.

"Anisha, would you like to hold Maya? She's been waiting to meet her big cousin. I've been telling her all about you! Come and sit here with us."

So I do, and even though I feel nervous because

she's so small, it feels nice to sit between Aunty Bindi and Uncle Tony.

"You know, she has Manny's hair and Mindy's eyes – but I think she has your smile," Aunty Bindi tells me.

"I don't know if that's true," I say, but I'm smiling the biggest smile anyway.

They put baby Maya in my lap and show me how to support her head, and I'm looking at her sleeping when the most unexpected thing happens. A big fat tear falls from my eye! And then I can't stop! Why am I crying?!

"Aw, are you okay, Anisha?" Aunty Bindi asks.

"Beta, what is it?" Mum asks.

"She's so beautiful and so tiny!" I say. "I just want to protect her and keep her safe."

Everyone cries then, but they're happy tears. And finally I feel part of it. Granny Jas picks Maya up and sings to her. Mum makes some tea and gets some snacks out, and we all sit around just enjoying being together. And it's not chaotic and there's no drama. It's just us all taking in the wonder of baby Maya.

I look around at my family. Things have changed so much recently, and our family has grown so much bigger.

Aunty Bindi is trying to take a selfie of everyone crammed onto the big sofa, but she can't quite get the angle. "I'll take it," I offer.

Mindy laughs. "No way, Anisha, you need to get over here and be in the picture."

She grabs my arm and pulls me into the centre of the group. I'm squished and the photo turns out all wonky, but I look at my family and I realize: I know exactly what part I play in this family. I know exactly where I belong, and it's right here, in the middle of the chaos and the too-tight cuddles.

I look at the baby, who is just falling asleep, and I whisper, "Hi, baby. I'm your big cousin Anisha. Don't worry, you'll get used to the noise. They're not so bad once you get to know them all, and I'll always be here for you."

The baby seems to understand me and falls asleep, contented in Uncle Tony's arms despite all the noise and Aunty Bindi insisting we take another photo.

"Hey, Anisha, you know what we should do?" Granny asks.

"What, Granny?" I ask. "Some calm reading time, maybe?"

"Ha! No, **beta**. We should take a family holiday abroad! I wonder... If I try again to take my pilot's test, maybe I could fly us!"

"What? That doesn't sound...I mean, that's a lovely idea, Granny, but, you know, I just don't think..."

But it's too late, Granny is already grabbing the laptop to look up flying lessons. I don't really like flying anyway, and I love Granny but I'm not sure we should put her in charge of a plane! Suddenly, Uncle Tony gets up and passes the baby to me.

"Back in a second," he says.

I'm just enjoying holding her when I get a strange whiff of something a bit pongy. In fact, that smell is pretty bad. I look around. Where is it coming from? I look down at baby Maya – it's not her, is it?

Manny comes to sit next to me and immediately holds his nose. **"WHAT IS THAT SMELL!"** he chokes.

I look around desperately for someone to take the baby, but they're all backing away slowly and grimacing.

I look down at Maya, who gurgles.

"I, er, I don't know how to change you, but I guess we could try," I tell her.

Luckily just at that moment Aunty Bindi takes her off me and says, "Don't worry, I'll sort this mischievous little munchkin out. Do you want to help, Anni?"

"Er, maybe next time," I say, trying not to heave as she starts to clean the baby up.

Granny suddenly jumps up excitedly, still holding the laptop – "I've found it!" – but as she does, she kicks the open nappy and it flies across the room, towards me!

MEET THE AUTHOR

Name: Serena Kumari Patel

Lives with: My brilliant family, Deepak, Alyssa and Reiss

Favourite Subjects: Science and History

Ambitions: To learn to ride a bike (I never learned as a kid).

To keep trying things I'm scared of.

To write lots more books.

Most embarrassing moment:

Singing in Hindi at a talent show and getting most of the words wrong. I hid in the loo after!

MEET THE ILLUSTRATOR

Name: Emma Jane McCann

Lives with: A mysterious Tea Wizard called Granny Goddy, a family of bats in the attic, and far too many spiders. (I promise I'm not a witch.)

Favourite thing to draw: Spooky stuff like Dracula's Den in Anisha's first adventure. (Still not a witch, honest.)

Ambitions: To master a convincing slow foxtrot.

Most embarrassing moment:

I used to collect old teacups and china. One day, I was in a teashop with a friend and the cup she was using was really pretty. I picked it up to check the maker's mark on the base, forgot it already had tea in it, and spilled the lot all over the both of us. (Witches are too cool to ever do anything like that.)

Keep an eye out for news on further adventures with ANISHA, ACCIDENTAL DETECTIVE, more from SERENA PATEL, and fabulously funny stories at usborne.com/fiction